Terrible eveni...
the wind.

Nate waited until the plane's propeller stopped chopping the air before he waded into the thigh-deep water. The pilot opened the door with a whoop of joy, which was entirely appropriate given the circumstances.

"Glad to see you, Hank. What on earth were you thinking?" Nate yelled.

The passenger door opened then. A woman, beautiful and amazingly composed, smiled at Nate. "I'm to blame, I'm afraid. I was so eager to get here I offered him triple his normal fee."

He knew that voice. He blinked. He knew…that face. Despite all the years that had passed, he knew it in an instant. Heart shaped, with a delicate nose, a pair of perfect lips and eyes as blue as Lake Huron's waters.

His gut clenched as time reeled backward. He was a teenager again, carefree, happy, in love…before having his heart brutally ripped from his chest.

"Holly?"

"It's been a long time."

Dear Reader,

What little girl doesn't dream of being a princess? I certainly did. As an adult, however, I can see how taxing it would be—all of those restrictions and obligations. All of those people depending on you to do and say the right thing. And to always be in the public's eye, via the media? No thank you.

Still, it was great fun to put myself in Princess Hollyn's fashionable high heels for a bit as a writer and imagine her brief reprieve from royal life as a tourist on fictional Heart Island.

Since I wrote this story in the dead of winter, it also was a joy to have a warm and sunny setting to immerse myself in—one far different from the snowy, subzero reality to be found outside my office window.

I hope you enjoy Holly and Nate's journey to happily-ever-after. As always, I'd love to hear what you think. Contact me through my website, www.jackiebraun.com.

Best wishes,

Jackie Braun

JACKIE BRAUN
The Princess Next Door

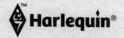

TORONTO NEW YORK LONDON
AMSTERDAM PARIS SYDNEY HAMBURG
STOCKHOLM ATHENS TOKYO MILAN MADRID
PRAGUE WARSAW BUDAPEST AUCKLAND

PLEASE RECYCLE · THIS PRODUCT IS RECYCLABLE

Recycling programs
for this product may
not exist in your area.

ISBN-13: 978-0-373-17767-7

THE PRINCESS NEXT DOOR

Published first in the U.K. under the title
CONFESSIONS OF A GIRL-NEXT-DOOR

First North American Publication 2011

Copyright © 2011 by Jackie Braun Fridline

Jackie Braun is a three-time RITA® Award finalist, a four-time National Readers' Choice Award finalist and a winner of the Rising Star Award for traditional romantic fiction. She can be reached through her website, www.jackiebraun.com.

"Heart Island is based on one of my favorite vacation destinations: Michigan's Drummond Island. It's the perfect place to leave real-world cares behind…and the fishing is good, too!"

Jackie Braun

To little princesses everywhere…

CHAPTER ONE

HOLLYN Elise Phillipa Saldani always did what was expected of her. As next in line for the throne of the tiny Mediterranean principality of Morenci, she'd known from an early age what her duties entailed and she'd followed them to the letter. Which was why her driver looked at her as if she were speaking a language other than the four in which she was fluent when she said, "Take me to the airport, please."

"The airport, Your Highness?" Henry asked.

She settled back in the plush leather seat of the limousine and fussed with the folds of her full skirt. Even though her heart was hammering, Hollyn said with characteristic calm, "Yes. The airport."

Henry wasn't mollified. He lifted one bushy eyebrow and inquired, "Are we picking up a passenger, then, on our way to the annual garden party? The queen didn't mention it."

No, indeed. Her mother hadn't mentioned it, because Olivia Saldani wasn't privy to Hollyn's last-minute change in plans.

"We are not picking up a passenger." Hollyn moistened her lips. This was it. There would be no turning back once she said the words. Once she gave the edict, her will would be done. "You are dropping one off. Me."

Henry cleared his throat. "I beg your pardon. I must not have heard you correctly."

"Yes, you did." Despite her nerves, she smiled. "Your hearing is as good now as it was when you caught me trying to take out the Bentley with cousin Amelia when I was sixteen."

"Your giggles gave you away, Your Highness."

She sighed. "It's just Hollyn."

But she hadn't been "just Hollyn" in too many years to count. Not to Henry or the other people who staffed the royal palace. Or the citizens of the small kingdom that she would one day rule. To them she was Princess Hollyn, daughter of King Franco and Queen Olivia, next in line to the Morenci throne and rumored to be soon engaged to the son of one of the country's most celebrated and dashing young businessmen.

Duty. She understood it and accepted it. But that didn't mean she liked it. Or that she didn't wish, sometimes, that she could be an ordinary young woman, living a simpler life.

Holly.

The nickname whispered from her past, beckoning from across the Atlantic. She allowed herself the luxury of recalling the boy who'd called her that. In her memory, a pair of wide-set brown eyes crinkled with a smile that also caused his cheeks to dent.

At fifteen, Nathaniel Matthews had been surprisingly self-assured and determined to break free of the small community the past two generations of his family had so eagerly embraced. She'd found the tiny island tucked between Canada and America in Lake Huron a paradise.

She'd spent five summers on Heart Island, so named because of its shape, living in anonymity and loving every minute of her unregimented life. No teas or cotillions to attend. No fussy state dinners. And no boring garden parties where more eyes would be focused on her than the blooms.

"The airport," she said again. "A plane is waiting for me."

Not the royal jet, but a private one she'd chartered for this trip. In the rearview mirror, she saw Henry's brows draw together. His perplexed expression was endearing and nostalgic. She remembered that look of concern from the days when he'd taught her to drive on the palace grounds. Afterward, she and Henry had laughed like a pair of loons at her exploits, which included an encounter with a bee-infested log. It was doubtful this day would end with much mirth.

"I'm leaving, Henry."

"Your mother never spoke of it."

Hollyn fussed with the folds of her skirt again. She couldn't wait to take it off and change into something less formal. "She doesn't know."

Those bushy brows drew together a second time. "But, Your Highness…"

She closed her eyes briefly, feeling swallowed up by a life that so many other young women in her kingdom considered a dream. For her, lately at least, it had become a nightmare.

"It's Hollyn. Please, Henry, just call me Hollyn."

When he stopped the car at a light, he turned with a tentative smile. "Hollyn."

Despite her best efforts to remain firm, her eyes filled with tears.

"I need a holiday, Henry. Just a few days, a week at the most, to be by myself. My life has been decided since before my birth, and now, with all of the pressure to accept Phillip's proposal…please." Her voice faltered.

Perhaps it was that more than her words that caused Henry to nod. After all, she was known for her stoicism.

"The airport," he said.

"Thank you."

"My pleasure." He sounded only marginally concerned when he asked, "And what am I to tell Her Majesty?"

Hollyn took a moment, drawing in a breath and working up the nerve to go against her mother's wishes. No one crossed Olivia without expecting retribution.

"You are to tell her that, at my command, you dropped me off at the airport. I have a letter for you to give to her that will explain my decision and my whereabouts. It also instructs her not to censure you in any way for carrying out my orders."

He smiled as he shook his head. "I'd do it anyway, you know."

She did.

Their gazes caught in the rearview mirror. "Thank you, Henry. I know this is an imposition."

He shrugged and pushed his trademark black cap back on his forehead. "I've never considered you an imposition, Hollyn."

Her eyes pooled with tears upon hearing her given

name, uttered this time without any prompting. But there was no time to give in to sentiment, even if Henry would have allowed it. They had arrived at the small country's only airport. Henry brought the limo around to a private entrance reserved for VIPs and royalty. They were shielded from prying eyes, although an industrious paparazzo or two had managed to breach security in the past. She held her breath, silently chanting, "Not today. Please, not today," as Henry unloaded the luggage she'd stowed, unbeknownst to him, in the limousine's trunk. He added to the trolley the three sleek designer bags whose contents she could barely remember packing, she'd done it so quickly. But then, where she was going, she wouldn't need much. No ball gowns, no ostentatious jewels or tiaras. As she recalled, shoes had been optional.

"I hope you find what it is you seek," he said softly once they were inside. Then he wrapped her in the kind of hug a father might, though her own wasn't one for displays of affection, whether in public or private.

"At the moment, Henry, all I seek is peace."

"Then that, my dear, is what I wish for you." He kissed her cheek and stepped away. "Write?"

The corners of her mouth turned up in a smile. "I won't be gone *that* long. As I said, a week at most."

He remained serious. "Be in touch when you can."

"Of course."

An hour later, as she settled into one of the plush seats of the private jet she'd chartered, she thought of her request.

Peace.

She might as well have been asking for the moon. But

with most of the paparazzi tied up at the annual garden party, and no one but Henry privy to her travel plans at this point, perhaps she would be able to make a clean getaway. She'd worry about a "clean arrival" once she got to where she was going.

Nate was seated on the deck of his home. He was finishing up a burger that he'd picked up from a local pub before heading home, and enjoying a cold beer when he spied the Cessna riding low on the horizon over Lake Huron.

Hell of an evening to land a seaplane, given the wind.

Even on the relatively protected waters of Heart Island's Pettibone Bay, whitecaps sent waves crashing on the beach with unrelenting precision. Forecasters were calling for a doozy of a storm, likely to hit sometime before midnight. The islanders, especially those along the coastline, were battened down, ready. Storms such as these weren't uncommon in summer, which was why people with any sense were already in for the night, their planes and boats secured to wait out the worst of the weather.

What in the hell was Hank Whitey thinking?

Sure, the pilot had a penchant for taking risks. Last week, he'd bluffed his way through their weekly poker game with a pathetic hand of cards. But Hank generally wasn't one to take risks with his plane; the aircraft was his livelihood.

Nate went inside, set his unfinished beer on the counter and headed out. Not only was he curious about Hank's explanation, but the man was also going to need a hand.

By the time Nate jogged down to the sand, Hank had already bypassed the dock at the Haven Marina, which was part of the resort Nate owned. On a really calm day, Hank might have moored there. Today, not a chance. The waves tossed the small plane around as if it weighed no more than a fishing bobber.

Nate would give Hank this. The guy was a capable pilot, even if his judgment was a bit questionable. Just beyond the plane, a jagged outcropping of rocks lined a slim finger of land that jutted to where a lighthouse stood. With the wind pushing toward those rocks, it took experience and skill to guide the Cessna toward the sandy beach instead.

Nate waited until the single engine was cut and the plane's propeller finally stopped chopping the air before he kicked off his shoes and waded out into the thigh-deep water. The waves made keeping his balance difficult and the cuffs of his shorts were wet in no time. Hank's door opened and the man let out a whoop of joy, which was entirely appropriate given the circumstances.

"You're damned lucky to be in one piece!" Nate shouted to be heard over the wind.

"Hey, Nate. Can't tell you how glad I am to see you."

"Glad to see you, too, Hank. Alive. What in the hell were you thinking?"

The passenger door opened then. A woman, beautiful and amazingly composed under the circumstances, smiled at Nate. "I'm to blame, I'm afraid. I was so eager to get here that I offered Mr. Whitey triple his normal fee."

Her crisp accent had Nate's brows tugging together. He knew that voice. He blinked. He knew…that face.

Despite all of the years that had passed, he knew it in an instant. Heart-shaped, with a delicate nose, a pair of perfect lips and eyes as blue as Huron's deepest waters.

His gut clenched as time reeled backward. He was a teenager again, carefree, happy, experiencing his first love…before having his heart brutally ripped from his chest.

"Holly?"

"It's been a long time."

She had the nerve to smile, which caused his teeth to clench. After all these years, he still felt betrayed, even if he also understood why she'd misled him. She hadn't owed him the truth.

That didn't stop him from wanting an explanation now. "Why are you here?"

Her smile disappeared. Her composure slipped. "I needed to get away. I needed…a holiday."

He could read between both the lines in her words and the one now denting the flesh between her eyes. She wanted normalcy. Anonymity.

That's what her American grandmother had been after, too, when she'd insisted Holly spend her summers on the island when she was a girl. From ages ten through fifteen, Holly and the older woman had shown up faithfully the second week in June and then stayed through the second week in August, renting the largest and most secluded of the resort's cottages.

He and Holly had become fast friends when she was ten and he was twelve. When she'd been fifteen to his seventeen, they'd had more on their minds than seeing who could swim the fastest to the floating dock out in front of his parents' house.

"So, you nearly killed Hank here? Well, I guess your wish is his command."

"I coulda said no, Nate," Hank argued, no doubt perplexed by the irritation in Nate's tone.

Nate was a little perplexed, too. This anger, these emotions, they belonged to the past. Yet he couldn't stop himself from adding, "No one says no to a princess, Hank"

The other man looked confused. Holly looked desperate. "I'm just an ordinary woman, Nate."

The wind gusted, and the waves slapped higher on his thighs. He decided to allow the distinction for now, even though he knew firsthand that nothing about her was ordinary. Hell, he'd known that to be the case even when he hadn't been privy to her true identity and royal lineage.

He waded the rest of the way to the plane's float. "Put your arms around my neck."

"Excuse me?"

Perversely, he enjoyed the fact that her eyes widened. *Nervous, Princess?* he wanted to ask. It would make him feel better to know that she was as shaken by this unexpected reunion as he was. Instead, Nate nodded in the direction of the shore. "Unless you'd rather walk to the beach, I'll carry you. I'm guessing those pretty shoes of yours probably aren't meant to get wet."

They were red leather flats with fat bows stretched across the toes. He could only guess what they cost. In her world, they would be considered casual. As would the understated linen suit she'd paired with them. In his, they would pass for Sunday best. If this was the kind of clothing she'd brought to blend in with the locals and the majority of tourists, she was going to stick out like a sore thumb.

"Right." She gave a quick dip of her chin before tilting it up. He remembered that defiant gesture from their childhood. She'd used it whenever he'd issued a dare.

"We don't have all day," he prodded when she hesitated. "I have to help Hank secure his plane for the night."

"I'm not staying," Hank called from the other side of the Cessna. "Got a card game waiting for me back on the mainland. Gerald's cousin is in town. Guy is damned unlucky at poker, but he bets like a Vegas high roller."

"You're staying," Nate disagreed. "One suicide mission an evening is enough. You can bunk at my place."

Hank cocked his head to one side as if considering. "Got any cold beer?"

"Yeah."

The other man shrugged. "I guess I can be persuaded. 'Sides, the guy's here through the weekend. I'll settle for picking *your* pocket at cards tonight."

Nate turned his attention back to Holly and held out his arms. She offered a tentative smile as she reached for him, and then she was in his embrace. She felt a little too good there, a little too perfect, with the side of her body pressed against his chest. Nate recalled the girl she'd been: long-limbed and lithe, verging on skinny. This was no girl he held. While she was still slender, during the intervening years she'd filled out nicely in all of the right places.

He started toward the shore, eager for the safety of the sand so that he could release her. Be free of her? Not likely. Until today, he'd thought he had been. Now? He was cursing his arrogance. She'd always been there, in the back of his mind.

His stride was purposeful, but perhaps a little too fast given the conditions and the added distraction of a beautiful woman in his arms. She had his hormones starting to lurch as powerfully as the surf. He stubbed his toe on a rock and managed to right his balance only to lose it again entirely when his other foot connected with another one.

"Nate!"

Holly's grip on his neck tightened to a choke hold as he veered from one side to the other. He tried to right himself, but it was too late. Momentum and waves were working against him. He knew a moment of utter defeat just before he toppled over, sending them both into the chilly, knee-deep water. It was too shallow for her to be submerged completely, but between the waves and the splash their bodies made going down, they were both good and soaked. The hair on one side of her head was slicked to her face. So much for the shoes he'd so chivalrously offered to help save from harm. They likely were as ruined as her oatmeal-colored pantsuit.

He expected outrage from her, perhaps even a good dressing down. She was a princess, after all. And he was but the owner of a small, albeit well-tended, resort.

But what he heard over the wind as Holly pushed to her feet was laughter. Unrestrained, boisterous laughter.

"That was smooth, Nathaniel. Yes, indeed. Very smooth." Grinning, she put out a hand, offering to help him up. She looked just then very much like the impish young girl who used to take such delight in playing pranks on him.

Nate felt like an idiot, and he knew he looked ridiculous. That didn't stop him from clasping her palm. Nor did it prevent him from joining in her mirth as he rose and shoved the hair back from his face. The situation *was* funny, even if it came at his expense.

Behind them, Hank was chortling away, too. Nate groaned. His reputation was toast. Unless he got lucky and the storm took out the phone lines and closed the locals' favorite tavern, news of this mishap would be the talk of the island before another sunset.

"Sorry about that. I lost my footing." As they reached the shore, he couldn't resist adding, "I might have maintained my balance, but you've put on a few pounds since we were kids."

Holly turned. Her mouth formed an indignant *O* as she thumped his chest with one small fist. "A gentleman isn't supposed to say such things to a lady."

Her words, even though they were said in jest, caused him to sober. She was more than a lady, she was a princess. Just that quickly, the gulf between their worlds gaped wide once more.

Hooking a thumb over his shoulder, he said, "I'd better go and give Hank a hand."

It took no more than fifteen minutes for Nate and the pilot to pull the plane ashore and beach it. Just to be on the safe side, they used the trunk of a big cedar tree that leaned toward the lake as a mooring. The Cessna wouldn't be going anywhere, despite the coming storm. Nate hoped the same could be said for all of the boats and the several large yachts moored at the resort's marina. Time would tell.

All the while, Holly waited patiently out of the way, soaked to the skin and shivering, but no complaints passed her lips. And he'd been expecting them. When her luggage was unloaded, her expression was one of chagrin.

"Just how long are you here for?" Nate asked, eyeing the trio of designer bags.

A pair of delicate shoulders rose in a shrug. "Perhaps as much as a week."

He ran his tongue over his teeth. "A week, hmm?" He could pack for a week in one small duffel, especially this time of year.

"I wasn't sure what I would need," she said.

For a moment he forgot that he was speaking to royalty. She was simply Holly. "Tank tops, shorts, a pair of comfortable walking shoes, maybe a hoodie for cool nights and a swimsuit would do."

"I packed those.... And a little bit more."

"So I see."

The contents of his closet could fit in those bags, but Nate decided to give her a break. After all, he'd been around enough women to know they had a whole different definition for the word *essentials*.

She reached for the smallest bag. It had wheels, not that they would do much good on the sand. "Sorry to be an imposition."

An interesting choice of words, to be sure.

"Where are you staying?" he asked.

Her expression brightened. "I'd hoped to rent the

cottage Gran and I always stayed in at your parents' resort."

"My parents are gone."

"Gone?" She looked alarmed.

"Retired," he clarified. "They moved to Florida four years ago." Just after he'd returned to the island from a job at one of the swankiest hotels in Chicago.

"The resort?"

Normally, it would give Nate great satisfaction to claim ownership and to admit that he'd expanded the place considerably since taking over. But this was *Princess* Hollyn Saldani. He doubted she would be impressed.

"I'm the owner now."

"Oh." One syllable that told him how enthused she was, but he'd give her this, she rallied fast. "I was hoping to find a place available."

"Sorry." He shook his head slowly, not sure whether he was relieved or disappointed. "We're all booked up at the moment. In fact, I don't know that there's a vacancy anywhere on the island until after the Fourth of July."

Usually, given how far north the island was, its resorts weren't full with patrons until after Independence Day. But this year, warm weather had come early and people from downstate were willing to make the drive and then the short ferry trip from Michigan's upper peninsula to the island.

"I wasn't thinking. I should have made arrangements ahead of time," she murmured. "Do you suppose there are any homes for rent on the island? I'd love to be on the water, of course, but I'll take what I can get at this point. Beggars can't be choosers."

It was an interesting statement coming from a woman who was next in line to the throne of her own kingdom.

"I don't know of anything offhand. You can check, but given the time of day and the storm, my guess is that most places are closed for the night." He snorted. "You know the island. Sidewalks pretty much roll up after eight o'clock."

He imagined she'd grown accustomed to glitzy, late-night parties with exclusive guest lists and the finest gourmet cuisine. Yet she didn't seem bothered by the prospect of no real nightlife here.

Her smile was nostalgic, damned near fond, when she replied, "Yes, I remember."

Was that *really* why she'd come?

Sure, she'd told him she needed to get away, but weren't there all sorts of fancy spas in Europe—and America, for that matter—more likely to fit the bill for a royal retreat than an out-of-the-way island that catered to the needs of middle-class tourists seeking good fishing, great scenery and a slower pace?

Hank reached them then, toting the last of her bags.

"Don't worry, miss. Nate's house has plenty of room. You can stay there at least for tonight." He glanced at Nate for corroboration.

What else could Nate do but nod? The quiet evening at home he'd envisioned just an hour ago now included two overnight guests. He knew from previous experience that Hank snored like a drunken sailor. Nate also knew that it was Holly who would keep him awake this night.

CHAPTER TWO

HOLLY wasn't sure what to do since Nate's invitation was begrudging at best.

That hurt. Not that she'd expected him to greet her with arms wide open. In fact, she hadn't been expecting to see him at all. She remembered how determined he'd been to leave the island for big-city living. But his displeasure right now was palpable, even if, for just a moment when they'd wound up sitting in the lake, he'd reminded her of the handsome young man who'd made her teenage pulse race with a simple smile.

As tempting as it was to turn down his offer, she had to be pragmatic. As she recalled, the island had a finite number of accommodations available. She would be lucky to find anything else on such short notice, so she followed him and the pilot up the beach.

Tomorrow, she could return to the mainland if need be. Tonight, she needed a place to stay. Jet lag was catching up with her. And that short flight over from the mainland had left her with white knuckles and a queasy stomach. In hindsight, she shouldn't have chanced it, especially this late in the day, with no firm reservation and a storm blowing in. She'd not only risked her life, but also the life of the pilot. A fact Nate had been only too happy to point out. Despite what he must think, it wasn't like Holly to be so thoughtless. But as with everything the past several days, desperation had her acting out of character.

Her hasty plan's imperfections were glaringly obvious now. She should have been more thorough in her arrangements before packing her bags and jetting across the Atlantic. That much was clear now. What had been as transparent as glass less than forty-eight hours ago was that she had to get away.

She caught up to Nate and glanced sideways at his stern profile. He wasn't exactly glad to see her. But it was her own emotions that gave her pause. She wasn't sure how she felt about seeing him again.

Once upon a time, she'd thought… Mentally, she shook her head. It was foolish to recall those dreams. They'd been unrealistic then. Now, they were unfathomable. Once again, she felt the grip of destiny tighten around her like a vise. There was no escaping it. Not completely, anyway, even if she hoped to find respite for a few days or a week. Holly groaned.

She didn't expect it to be heard over the wind, but Nate turned and asked, "Something wrong?"

"No."

"No?" His brows rose.

His wry expression and disbelieving tone came as a bit of a surprise. Back home no one would have dared to question her—well, except for her mother, who browbeat Holly regularly over the most minute of things. Holly needed to be perfect. Or at least give the illusion of perfection at all times. Interestingly, coming from

Nate, she rather enjoyed it. She'd much rather he treated her as an equal, even one with whom he was angry.

They reached the house, a cedar-sided bungalow that she remembered from her visits to the island as a girl. Back then, he'd lived in it with his parents, and she'd always been welcome inside for a bite to eat or to watch the telly on a rainy afternoon. His mother, she recalled, had been amazingly tolerant of such things as sandy feet and soggy swimsuits.

From the outside, the place looked much the same except for a newer and larger deck that wrapped around to the side entrance. Hank beat them up the steps and shucked off his shoes before opening the squeaky-hinged screen door and going in. That left Holly and Nate standing on either side of the welcome mat.

Nothing about Nate's demeanor at the moment was very welcoming.

"This is too much of an imposition," she began. It definitely was too much of something.

"It's fine," Nate insisted. "No big deal." He toed off his soggy shoes and pushed them against the side of the house next to Hank's battered sneakers.

"I'll pay—"

"It's only one night, Holly…Hollyn…Princess…." He shoved his damp hair back from his forehead in agitation. "What am I supposed to call you?"

From his tone, she imagined he already had a pet name or two in mind. "Holly is fine."

She *wanted* to be just Holly again. That was, after all, why she'd made this rash trip in the first place.

He looked doubtful, but nodded. "I insist you stay, all right? As my guest."

His words might have been more reassuring had they not been issued through clenched teeth. But any retort she might have offered was lost when he reached for the back of his damp T-shirt and pulled it over his head.

Holly swallowed hard, but that didn't keep her mouth from watering. As a teenage girl, she'd admired Nate's form. He'd been wiry then, lean and several inches shorter than the six foot three she judged him to be now. He'd shot up, filled out. Quite obviously, he worked out. A sculpted abdomen such as his was no happy accident of genetics.

"Your turn."

His words startled her. She felt her cheeks grow warm, though it wasn't only embarrassment that caused the building heat.

"I beg your pardon?"

"Your shoes. If you wouldn't mind, take them off out here."

Half of his mouth crooked into a wry smile as he draped his shirt over the banister. He was enjoying her discomfort, enjoying that she was as off balance now as he'd been while wading through the surf earlier.

Holly glanced down at her feet. The shoes he'd tried to spare damage with his chivalrous offer to carry her ashore were not only wet, but also covered in sand and other natural debris from their trek over the beach.

"Your mother never minded the sand."

"She did, but she was too polite to say so. Regardless, since I clean the place now, I make the rules."

"Right." Envisioning him with a mop in one hand and a feather duster in the other helped take some of the sting out of his words.

She did as Nate asked and padded inside behind him.

Hank already had made himself at home on the couch in front of the television. His stocking feet were propped up on the coffee table, a long-necked brown bottle was in one hand and the remote control was in the other. A baseball game was on. Holly didn't know much about the American pastime, but she'd always enjoyed listening to the announcers explaining what was going on. Their voices were so soothing, spiking here and there as warranted by a key play. The sound made her nostalgic. As did the house, even though the furnishings now were more masculine and sparse than the fussy decor that had obviously been Mrs. Matthews's taste.

Gone were the knickknacks and kitschy collections that had filled two curios cabinets. Gone was the mauve-and-blue color scheme, the lace curtains and flowered camelback sofa. Now the main living area sported top-of-the-line electronics, a brown leather sectional and some surprisingly high-quality pieces of artwork, all of them seascapes.

Nate must have noticed the direction of her gaze. "Rupert Lengard," he said, supplying the name of the artist. "I wish I could say they're originals, but they're limited edition prints."

"They're stunning." She pointed to one. "That looks like that little island we used to take the canoe out to."

They'd pretended to be castaways and had even tried to erect a tree house à la the Swiss Family Robinson. But getting building supplies over in the canoe had proved too much of a hassle. They'd made do with a lean-to crafted from sticks and cedar boughs.

"Horn Island," Nate said. "Lengard spent a couple summers on Heart and the surrounding islands. All of the prints I bought are local scenes."

She admired the subject matter as much as the artist's obvious skill. "I'll have to see about getting some of them for home."

"His stuff is not exactly on par with Poussin or Renoir."

Apparently, Nate thought only work of old-world masters would suit her sensibilities. Holly decided to set him straight. "My tastes run a little more modern than that. Like you, I buy art, whether prints or originals, because I like it, not because of the value an insurance appraiser might put on it."

Nate nodded curtly. It sounded like he might have said, "Touché."

But he was already turning away and heading over to the couch.

"Anything else I can get you, Hank?" Nate asked dryly.

The other man either missed the sarcasm or chose to ignore it. "You got anything to munch on? Like nachos maybe?"

Holly hid her grin.

"You want nachos?"

Hank dragged his gaze from the television. His expression was hopeful. "Yeah."

"They sell them down at the Fishing Hole Tavern. Bring back an order for me, too, while you're at it," Nate replied before using his shin to knock the other man's feet off the table. To Holly, he said, "Follow me. I'll show you to your room."

He went back to grab her bags from their spot by the door and started for the stairs. At the top, he turned right and continued to the room at the end of the hall.

She stood uncertainly at the threshold after he entered. "But th-this is your room."

And it was just as she recalled it, though she hadn't spent much time in it as a girl. His parents wouldn't have allowed that, especially once she and Nate were teenagers.

Even though they were both adults now, she felt awkward and oddly aware. She blamed it on the fact that he was shirtless and she was...tired. Really, really tired.

"Not anymore. I have the master these days. After my folks moved out I did a little renovation work and added an en suite bathroom, so the one in the hall is all yours." His brows rose in humor. "Well, yours and Hank's. You'll have to share."

He set down her bags and crossed to open the window a few inches. He repeated the process for the one on the opposite wall. The wind rushed inside, ruffling the edges of the curtains and bringing with it the mingled scents of cedar trees and wood smoke. She recalled that earthy scent from those summers long past. Nostalgia had her smiling. A lot of fireplaces would be in use tonight if the temperature outside continued to drop. Her gaze veered to Nate and her smile disappeared. Holly wasn't feeling chilled. Quite the opposite. Even wearing wet clothes, all it took was an eyeful of the taut muscles that defined Nate's shoulders, and she had to fight the urge to fan herself.

He turned around to find her studying him. God only knew what her expression revealed. He was one of the few people around whom she had ever been herself, which was ironic, she realized now, since he hadn't known her actual identity.

She folded her hands at her waist, cleared her throat and said the first thing she could think of. "It's windy outside."

"The storm."

"Yes. The storm."

They eyed one another for a moment longer. "You can close the windows in a minute. Just give the place a chance to air out. It's a little stuffy in here. This room doesn't get much use."

A little stuffy? She could hardly breathe. But that had nothing do with stagnant air. It had everything to do with the way he was looking at her. She saw speculation in his gaze and, she thought, guarded interest. It dawned on Holly then that she must look a fright. Her soggy clothes were molded to her body, her makeup was nonexistent, and her hair... She reached up to run a hand through it only to have her fingers tangle in the snarls.

She pulled her hand free and managed to say, "It's fine."

He didn't appear convinced. In fact, he was shaking his head. "You know, the more I think of it, you belong in the master suite. You'd definitely be more comfortable in there."

He reached for her bags. She put out a hand to stop him. "Don't be silly. This is fine," she said again.

"It's not up to the standards you're used to," he said quietly.

"I'm not picky, Nathaniel." She went with his full name, hoping to get a rise out of him.

His gaze connected with hers. "You're a princess."

Holly folded her arms over her chest and the ache she felt building there. "You say it like it's some sort of disease."

"I'll apologize for that. But the fact remains, you're used to better than…this." He glanced around as if seeing the room for the first time. Clearly, he found it lacking. His gaze returned to her. "You're used to better than anything I have to offer, for that matter."

"Nate."

Before she could protest further, he was at the door, his hand on the knob. This time, his gaze didn't quite meet hers. "I'll leave you to freshen up. We can discuss your accommodations later."

The door closed. Holly stared at the scratched wood for a long time afterward. What had just happened? In the span of the past half hour, he'd gone from being smug and a little indignant to being uncomfortable and, unless she missed her guess, embarrassed. That wasn't the Nathaniel Matthews she remembered. He'd been fearless, formidable and a touch arrogant at times.

He'd been determined to take on the world. He'd seen no limit to the possibilities life had to offer him. She'd admired his conviction that he could be anything, do anything, go anywhere and answer to no one but himself. For a while, Holly had even begun to think like he did. Then she'd returned to Morenci, after what turned out to be her last summer on the island, and her mother had set her straight.

"You're no longer a child, Hollyn. You'll turn sixteen soon. It's time for you to fully embrace your royal responsibilities. You're a princess. You need to start acting like one at all times."

Her girlhood dreams had been dashed.

What, she wondered now, had made Nate change his plans? Or was it simply a case of growing up? After all, he'd been a boy when she'd known him.

Well, one thing was clear. The man who'd just closed the door was a stranger, even if so many things about him seemed familiar.

Nate changed into dry clothes and headed downstairs. In the kitchen, he pulled a fresh bottle of beer from the fridge, uncapped it and took a liberal swig.

God! What must she think of him? He probably came off as backward and irascible. He hadn't exactly rolled out the welcome mat upon learning she was Hank's passenger.

Welcome mat. He grunted now and took another gulp of beer. She was used to red carpets, state dinners and probably parades held in her honor. He'd even botched his attempt to carry her to shore. Still, she'd laughed. And in that moment he'd glimpsed the girl she'd been. The girl who at first had been his fishing buddy and who, later, when he was teenager, had kept him awake and confused on hot summer nights.

Now she was a woman. A beautiful woman. Staying under his roof. And, even though his parents were a couple thousand miles away enjoying their retirement and unable to act as chaperones, Holly was as off-limits as she'd been when his hormones had been raging as a teen. Hank sauntered into the kitchen then. They did have a chaperone after all. Nate couldn't make up his mind whether to be grateful or not.

"Where's Holly?" The other man's beer was empty. He helped himself to a fresh one from the fridge, shooting the cap in the direction of the trash can in the corner.

"Upstairs, probably getting out of her wet clothes." It was the wrong thing to say, Nate decided, when his imagination kicked into overdrive.

"I didn't realize you two knew one another. She didn't mention it on the flight over."

"We don't. Well, not really." Nate shrugged. Since Hank was waiting for more of an explanation, he added, "We spent several summers together when we were kids. It's been years since I last saw her."

That wasn't quite true since all he'd had to do in the interim was pick up a magazine or turn on the television and more times than not there was a feature on Morenci's future monarch. But then his Holly and Hollyn Saldani had always seemed like separate people to him. Until today. Today he was having a hard time keeping them straight.

"She looks familiar," Hank was saying.

Nate chose not to reveal Holly's secret. It was only because the pilot had the loosest lips in three counties, he told himself, and she'd already made it clear she'd come here to get away from the public eye. Besides, the last thing Nate wanted was for his peaceful little island to be overrun with journalists and paparazzi and royal gawkers. That would be bad for business.

Liar, a voice whispered. He ignored it. On a shrug, he replied, "I know. She has one of those faces."

Hank seemed satisfied with the answer, but he was still curious. "Where's she from? I know she's not American. She has an accent of some sort even though she speaks really good English."

Again, rather than lie outright, Nate chose to be vague. "Abroad somewhere. But some of her family vacationed in these parts."

He frowned after saying so. Had it really been her grandmother that she'd come to the island with? Or had the older woman been some sort of governess? He still had so many questions about the woman who had been his first love…and a total stranger.

The laid-back pilot appeared to accept the explanations Nate offered. Of course, Hank was easy to please. He had free, ice-cold beer, a place to sleep for the night and cable television, assuming the storm didn't knock it out.

Nate thought that was the end of their discussion of Holly, until the guy commented, "She sure is a pretty thing."

Nate swigged his beer and mumbled a response.

"And generous." Hank grinned. "You wouldn't believe what she paid me to fly her here."

"You were risking your life," Nate reminded him dryly.

The other man laughed loudly. "Maybe so, but neither of my ex-wives thought my life was worth that much."

The other man's attitude rubbed Nate the wrong way. "Well, it's easy to be generous when you've done nothing to earn the money in your wallet."

"She's loaded?"

Nate shrugged. "Her family's well-to-do. Old money." Really old money and a pedigree that could be traced back through the generations.

"Is she single?"

His gut clenched. "Far as I know." Though rumors were circulating in the media that an engagement was in her future. The first time Nate had heard them aired on a news program he'd not just been angry, he'd felt a little sick to his stomach. Neither reaction made sense. Nor did his reaction upon seeing her today.

"Imagine that. Pretty, single and rich." The other man pushed back his mop of unkempt salt-and-pepper hair. "Think I stand a chance?"

"Sorry, pal." Nate clinked the neck of his beer bottle against the one in Hank's hand in seeming commiseration. "I think she's out of your league."

Hank didn't appear overly troubled by the assessment. "What about yours?"

"Definitely."

Nate studied the bottle's label after he said it. He'd done all right for himself in life. In fact, he was quite pleased by how far he'd come.

After high school graduation, he'd gone on to college. Nothing Ivy League, but his grades had been good enough to get him into a Big Ten school. He'd made the dean's list all four years at the University of Michigan. After earning a bachelor's degree, he'd moved to Chicago and had taken a management position at one of the hotels on the Miracle Mile.

His parents had been proud of him, though their unspoken disappointment that he hadn't wanted to take over the family resort had been clear. But they'd given him space and offered him choices. And after four years in the Windy City, he realized how much he missed the slow pace of life on the island. He missed the quiet mornings and spectacular sunrises on Lake Huron. When he'd packed up his belongings and left the island, he'd been so sure he wanted big-city living—the decadent nightlife, the pricey condo overlooking Navy Pier, the designer-label clothes and gourmet restaurants.

Everything had been great for a while, even if he'd still felt more like a tourist than a resident. He'd enjoyed making a name for himself. He'd enjoyed hearing the praise from his boss, and the predictions from corporate that he would be another rung up the ladder soon, maybe even managing a hotel of his own.

Then his parents had announced their retirement and their plans to sell Haven Resort & Marina. They wanted to move south to warmer climes. Nate had been pole-axed. Oh, he'd expected them to retire at some point. It wasn't as if they hadn't talked about it over the years. And he'd long known they had their eye on a condo on Florida's Gulf Coast. The winters on the island could be brutal and long, especially on achy, aging joints. But talking and doing were two different things.

Confronted by reality, he'd come to a couple of conclusions. One, he didn't want to live in Chicago. It was a great city, full of energy and excitement, but it wasn't for him. Not long-term, anyway. And two, he didn't want anyone but him to own the resort that his grandparents had started from nothing during the 1950s.

So, he'd gone home, not with his tail tucked between his legs, but confident that he'd made the right decision. He'd never regretted coming back. In fact, he'd been damned pleased with the changes he'd made, and those he continued to implement to bring the property up-to-date so that it would appeal to the needs of a new generation of tourists. The marina and outbuildings were in good shape. And he was renovating the cottages as money permitted. He'd completed half of them already, doing much of the work himself in the off-season. Gone were the mismatched furnishings and bedding, the ancient appliances and worn vinyl flooring. What he'd replaced them with weren't high-end, but they were durable, fresh, contemporary and comfortable. And the cottages now sported neutral color schemes and even some artwork from a local woman who specialized in nature views. They weren't as good as the ones captured by Lengard, but they complemented the decor and had helped bring some commissions the young artist's way.

Last year he'd added Wi-Fi and cable television, and he'd partnered with a local couple to offer guided hikes through the huge swath of federally owned land on the northern tip of the island that was home to all sorts of wildlife, including a couple of endangered bird species. In the spring, when the morel mushroom hunters came, he'd joined forces with one of the island's restaurants for cooking demonstrations. In addition to families and fishermen, his resort now appealed to naturalists and others embracing a greener lifestyle.

Winters were still pretty quiet. Only the heartiest of tourists ventured north during that time of year. But already he was making plans to attract more snowshoers, cross-country skiers and snowmobilers, which was why he had purchased another dozen acres of land just beyond what he owned now with plans to add trails and maybe even a few more cabins down the road.

His parents were impressed with the changes he'd made, even though he'd suggested most of them while they still owned the place. But the status quo had been good enough for them. He'd understood and accepted that. But within days of the transfer in ownership, he'd rolled up his sleeves and begun the transformation.

Now, business was up. Not just for his resort, but for other establishments on the island, thanks to a joint marketing campaign that he'd spearheaded. The head of the local chamber of commerce hadn't been pleased, since Nate basically had gone around Victor Montague's back. But everyone else was happy with the results.

Yes, he was proud of what he'd accomplished. Proud of what he'd made not only of the resort, but also of his life. Which was why it galled him to find himself glancing around his kitchen, another of his renovation projects, and wondering what Holly thought of his quaint home and simple life.

"Nate?" Hank gazed at him quizzically.

After another swig of beer, he muttered, "Definitely, she's out of my league."

Holly stood at the base of the steps. She hadn't intended to eavesdrop on Nate's conversation with Hank, but it was hard not to hear the men. The house was small. Their voices carried.

Out of his league?

She supposed she could understand how Nate would think that. He wasn't the first person, man or woman, who had acted as if she were made of priceless spun glass. A number of her childhood friends had become overly deferential and awkward around her once they had finally grasped her status as their future monarch. She recalled how isolated it had made her feel. How utterly lonely.

"That's just the way it is," her mother had told her matter-of-factly when she complained. "They treat you differently because you are different. You're special, Hollyn."

Holly hadn't wanted to be "special." She'd wanted friends. True friends who wouldn't purposely lose at board games or let her pick the movie every time they got together. Friends who would confide their secrets. Friends in whom she could confide hers and not risk having her private thoughts written up in the tabloids. That had happened when she was fourteen. She'd complained about an argument with her mother, who'd felt Holly was too young to wear makeup. The headline in the *Morenci Daily* two days later read: "Queen and her teen nearly come to blows over mascara."

Her mother had been livid. Holly had been crushed, and, hence forward, very, very careful.

After that, the closest she'd had to actual girlfriends were her cousins, Amelia and Emily. As the second and third in line for the throne behind Holly, they understood what it was like to be in the spotlight, photographed, quoted—or misquoted as the case may be—and constantly judged on their appearance and breeding as if they were entries in the Royal Kennel Club's annual dog show.

Yet, even with Amelia and Emily, the older they grew, the more she sensed a distance and a separation between them. And, yes, she could admit now, she'd noticed a certain amount of envy and bitterness that while Holly would have a prime place in Morenci's history books, their lives would be mere footnotes and largely forgotten.

Their emotional defection had hurt. But not as badly as overhearing Nate's assessment of her. He made her sound shallow, spoiled.

Spending money she hadn't earned?

As far as Holly was concerned, she was always "earning" her keep. Long ago, her life had ceased to be her own, if indeed it ever had been. She was public property. Her photograph was sold to the highest tabloid bidder, in addition to being plastered on everything from teacups, decorative plates and biscuit tins to T-shirts and tote bags that were then gobbled up by tourists.

She told herself the disappointment she felt about Nate's assessment of her was because she had so hoped to feel "normal" here. She had hoped to be treated as she had been treated as a girl coming to the island with her grandmother: Accepted for who she was rather than the crown she would someday wear.

A small sigh escaped. She was being foolish.

At least Nate hadn't told Hank the truth about her identity. If it meant letting the other man and the rest of the folks on the island think she was some snobby socialite eager for a taste of the simple life, so be it. Anonymity in itself was a gift. One that she hadn't enjoyed in more than a decade.

The men came out of the kitchen, both of them stopping with almost comedic abruptness when they spied her. Nate looked guilty, his gaze cutting away a moment before returning to hers. No doubt, he was wondering how much she'd overheard.

Hank, however, was grinning broadly.

"Hey, there, miss. I see you're none the worse for wear after your unexpected dip in the lake." He elbowed Nate in the ribs.

Nate flushed. So did she. Holly hardly looked her best. She'd changed into dry clothes, but they were wrinkled from their time spent in her bag. And while she'd combed the tangles out of her hair, it was still wet. She'd remembered a blow dryer in her hasty packing job, but she hadn't thought to bring an adapter. And, of course, she smelled of lake water.

She fiddled with the ends of her hair.

"I wanted to take a shower, but I'm afraid I couldn't figure out how to work the faucet so that the spray would come out."

"It's finicky," Nate said. "I should have thought to show you before coming downstairs."

"That's all right."

"I can show you now."

"Thank you. Oh, and I wasn't sure what to do with my wet things." She'd hung them over the shower curtain in the bathroom.

"I can toss them in the dryer."

She nibbled the inside of her cheek. The pants and jacket were both made of linen. The blouse was silk. "I don't suppose the island has a dry cleaners?"

Nate shook his head.

"The town on the mainland does," Hank supplied. "It's right next to the grocery store. I can take them with me when I fly back tomorrow and drop them off for you."

"Oh, that's all right. I don't want to be a bother." She added an appreciative smile.

"It's no trouble. None at all," he insisted.

This was exactly the sort of deferential treatment she was used to…and did not want. "I'll think about it," she answered diplomatically.

"Come on. I'll show you how to work the shower," Nate said, as if sensing her unease.

She followed him back up the stairs to the bathroom, hurriedly snatching a pair of white silk panties and a delicate lace-edged bra from the curtain rod and hiding them behind her back.

Nate coughed. They both smiled uncomfortably.

"Um, about the shower. You, uh, turn this knob." He demonstrated as he instructed. "The farther right you turn it, the hotter it becomes." She was thinking something on the cool side. "You'll probably want it somewhere in the middle. Then you flip this little lever on the side."

Again, he demonstrated. The water sprayed out from the showerhead. Small beads of it ricocheted off the tiled surround and landed on his forearm. The hair there was bleached as light as some of the streaks on his head, alluding to his time spent in the sun. Indeed, he had a good tan going. In comparison, Holly was ridiculously pale. It had been that way when they were kids, too, although by the end of her visit, she'd always managed to look like a regular beachcomber—or a commoner, as her mother complained.

No doubt Olivia had worked herself into a good fit

by now, despite the note of explanation that Henry had delivered on Holly's behalf. She felt a little guilty, a little queasy. And a lot rebellious, because she wasn't going to return for at least a week. Maybe longer. And even though her mother considered her engagement to Phillip a done deal, Holly was far from convinced.

Nate turned off the shower and stepped back. She glanced away.

"Everything okay?"

She pushed away all thoughts of her mother, Phillip and the responsibilities waiting for her upon her return. She was free now.

"I didn't see the lever," she said quietly.

"No one does. It's old-fashioned, which is why I had them all replaced in the cottages when I took over. Saved me or whoever else was manning the front desk at the marina office a lot of phone calls." He tucked his hands into his pockets. "I haven't gotten around to this one yet."

"I'm sure it hasn't been a priority."

"Not exactly," he agreed. "I've put most of my time and resources into the cottages."

"Walking up from the beach, it looked like there were more of those than there used to be."

He nodded. "I was always after Dad to expand, but he said he and Mom had enough to keep them busy with what they had."

"I liked your parents." She smiled, enveloped in simple and homey memories so unlike the majority of those from her childhood. That, too, she realized now, was part of the reason she'd come here. Simplicity. Her complicated, overrun life yearned for it. "They always made feel at home when I stopped over from my grand-mother's cottage, even when they had work to do and guests to attend to."

"They liked you, too. They were always after me to be as polite as you were."

They both laughed. Then sobered. Silence stretched. For a moment, given the way he was watching her, she thought he might stroke her cheek. He'd raised his hand. But it fell away and he blurted out, "Fresh towels."

Holly blinked.

"Um, for your shower. They're in the cabinet next to the sink. Washcloths, too."

"Right."

"One more thing, Holly."

She nodded, feeling ridiculously expectant as she waited for him to continue.

"Don't flush the toilet right before you get in the shower or you'll wind up scalded." He cleared his throat. His cheeks grew pink. "Another of those things I haven't gotten around to updating."

CHAPTER THREE

THE storm was in full swing by the time Holly came downstairs an hour later. Rain pelted the windows and lightning illuminated the inky sky, followed by loud crashes of thunder that shook the home's foundation.

It was a spectacle to behold, by turns frightening and thrilling. Even so, Hank was sprawled out on the couch, his snores competing with the storm. She envied the man's ability to fall asleep so easily. Even on perfectly quiet nights, Holly seldom slept soundly. She usually had too much going through her mind to relax and simply drift off. She'd tried the old remedies, such as counting sheep and listening to soothing music. Neither had much effect. Meditation sometimes worked. As did reading really, really boring accounts of her country's gross domestic product.

The royal physician blamed her insomnia on anxiety and had prescribed pills that she rarely took. They made her too groggy the next day, as if she were walking through a fog. She preferred to have her wits about her, even if it meant slumbering off sometimes during a dinner party. A picture of her with her eyes closed and her chin resting on her chest had graced the front page of a newspaper not long ago.

"This is exactly the kind of publicity you need to avoid," her mother had warned. "Royal or not, the press can turn public sentiment against you in a heartbeat."

Even so, Holly had been reluctant to take the pills. Still, she wondered if she would come to regret not bringing them with her for this trip.

Nate stood at the glass door that opened to the deck, one hand in the front pocket of a pair of wrinkled cargo shorts, the other holding a beer. He'd taken a shower. She'd heard the water in his bathroom running not long after she'd shut off the water in the guest bath. His hair was still wet. He wore it on the long side, though not as long as he had as a boy. Back then, it had nearly brushed his shoulders. Now, it just grazed his collar. The color had gotten darker over the years. It bordered on brown, but the sun had left its mark with the kind of highlights that women—and some men—spent vast sums of money at salons hoping to achieve. She couldn't imagine him sitting still long enough to let a stylist work her magic.

"It's impolite to stare, you know."

Too late she realized that he'd been watching her reflection in the glass.

"Yes. It is. I apologize."

She crossed to where he stood. Just as she reached his side, a bolt of lightning zigzagged across the sky, followed closely by a deafening boom. She jumped. Nate's arm shot out, encircling her waist. Then Hank snorted and they broke apart, both of them turning to watch the pilot as he stirred, but only enough to roll over on the couch. He didn't wake.

"He sleeps like the dead," Nate remarked, taking a pull of his beer. He seemed to remember his manners then. "Can I get you something to drink?"

A cup of freshly brewed tea would have been lovely. And way too much trouble. She nodded toward the beverage in his hand. "A beer, please."

His brows arched in doubt. "A beer?"

"That is what you're drinking."

"Uh-huh. It's a beer." He stated the obvious, clearly expecting her to change her mind.

"Then that's what I'll have. Please."

"Okay," he said, sounding none too convinced. But he went to the kitchen. He returned a moment later with a second long-necked bottle. Before handing it to her, he paused. "I'll get you a glass."

"No need. I can drink out of a bottle." Before he could protest, she took a sip.

This American beer was less robust than the ales favored in her country, but she liked the taste. Even more, she liked the seeming normalcy of drinking a beer from a bottle and watching a storm roll over the big lake.

"I'd forgotten how fierce the thunderstorms here can be."

"They pack a lot of punch," he agreed. "It has to do with the water. They tend to pick up steam moving over the Great Lakes. The good news is they usually pass as quickly as they come."

"I remember. Tomorrow, when we wake up, it will be like it never happened," she murmured.

But Nate was shaking his head. "There will be plenty of fallout. And I'll be out there cleaning up the debris. Everything has consequences, Holly."

"Are we still talking about the storm?"

He shrugged.

"You're angry with me." She said it as a statement rather than a question.

"Angry?" The corners of his mouth turned down in denial. "Why would I be angry? I mean, who am I to be angry?"

"Don't." She plucked at the edges of the label on the beer bottle. "I wanted to tell you who I was, Nate."

"But you didn't." Despite his claim that he wasn't angry, it was obvious in his tone.

"No. I didn't."

"Why?"

She sucked in a breath, memories of those carefree summers making her want to sigh. At last, she said, "I didn't want things to change. I wanted to be just Holly."

"You were never just Holly." His tone was as low and ominous as the storm.

"I was," she insisted. "Here, on this island, for all of those blissful summers, I was just Holly. I can't tell you how much I looked forward to coming to Heart each year. I started counting down the days just after the New Year. I didn't have any obligations when I was here. This was every bit the haven your resort's name proclaims it to be."

But Nate was shaking his head. "It was a fantasy," he insisted.

"All right." She wouldn't parse words. "It was a fantasy. But I needed it, Nate. Desperately."

She still did. He didn't know what it was like. How utterly on display she'd always felt back in her country. So little had been private, especially since her mother had insisted on granting the media unprecedented access.

Holly's first birthday? The cameras had been rolling, the entire party nationally televised so that everyone in Morenci could ooh and aah as the little princess messily gobbled up cake, opened her presents and then toddled on shaky legs around the palace garden. Sure, it had served as a fundraiser for a leading birth-defects charity, but still, it had set the tone. Every birthday, every milestone after that, had been open to the public via the media.

It was tiring to be smiling for the cameras at all times. It left very little room for one to be oneself. Sometimes, Holly felt like a fraud. She wasn't always happy or poised or eager to share her attention with whomever was demanding it.

Heaven help her, but sometimes she wanted to be selfish and irritable, maybe stamp her feet in protest or outrage or just because she was having a bad day. Perhaps even raise her voice or slam a door or break a dish. As if… She nearly laughed, just thinking of how outrageous such things would be. She hadn't been allowed the luxury of a tantrum.

But then, a couple of weeks ago, the idea of packing her bags and taking off unannounced had seemed outrageous and undoable. Perhaps there was hope for her after all.

Holly glanced at Nate. Given his rigid posture, she half expected him to disagree. Instead, he nodded slowly.

"I guess I can understand that."

"You can?"

He turned to face her. "After college, I worked in a very upscale hotel in Chicago. We catered to a lot of celebrity clientele. I know actors and rock stars aren't quite the same as royalty."

"Close enough," she murmured.

"Yeah. Well, I realized pretty quickly that their life-style wasn't always as glamorous as it seemed to much of their adoring public."

"It's not," she agreed softly. She scratched at the bottle's label again with one of her nails and frowned. "Everyone thinks they know you."

He turned. "I didn't know you at all."

"Nate—"

He was already facing the window again as he added, "Anyway, with all those pushy managers, obsessed fans and paparazzi trying to get to them twenty-four seven, I figured out pretty quickly that it's got to be annoying."

"There's very little privacy." Thinking again of her mother's open-palace-door policy, she added, "Very little."

"Yet you managed it for five summers."

Her lips curved at the memories.

"You know, running around in shorts and bathing suits, with my hair pulled into crooked pigtails, I didn't look very much like a princess. I think that's why I got away with it." She laughed ruefully. "Now, had I been wearing my royal tiara…"

As jokes went, it fell abominably flat. Nate wasn't amused. Far from it, if his tone were any indication.

"I felt like an idiot for not figuring it out. Holly… Hollyn." A snort escaped as he glanced her way. He raised his beer, took a sip. His gaze still on her, he said, "You must have thought I was pretty dense, especially those last couple of summers."

"No, Nate. Never. Honestly. I thought you were…" *Perfect. Gorgeous. My one true love.* She felt herself blush.

He apparently thought he had his answer. "You did."

"No. You were…my best friend."

Even before the words were out, Holly was calling herself a liar. He'd been so much more than that. Of course, she'd been fifteen years old at the time, flush with hormones and full of girlish fantasies about the future she and Nate would have together. A future that could never be.

"I missed you, Nate."

Her whispered words surprised them both.

It was a moment before he said, "That first summer you didn't show up on Heart, I all but haunted the cabin where you used to stay with your grandmother. I was sure you were just late. But guest after guest arrived and none of them was you. My parents finally started telling me in advance who had rented the place. It was getting embarrassing, I guess."

Beyond wryness, was that pain she heard in his

voice? It was selfish of her to hope so. Nonetheless, she did, recalling how she'd begged her mother to let her go and, then, begged her grandmother to intervene again.

"I can't, my girl," the older woman had told her. "It's time for you to accept your destiny. But I hope you'll never forget who you really are."

How ironic that all these years later, Holly still wasn't sure.

"So, was she really your grandmother? For a while, after I found out the truth, I thought maybe she was just another part of your cover."

"No." Her smile was fond. "She was really my gran."

"Your mother's mom," he guessed. "Now that I think of it, she had a bit of a Texas accent."

"As does my own mother, when she allows it to slip. Which is rare." Holly frowned. "She put her past behind her." Feeling disloyal, Holly added, "She wasn't exactly accepted in Morenci at first, despite her position." Every misstep and gaffe had been fodder for the gossip mill. The old guard was appalled that a Texas beauty queen had snagged their bachelor king.

"That must have been difficult for her."

"It was." It also was the reason Holly had given her mother as much free rein with her life as she had. She knew how hard Olivia had tried to fit in. How much she had sacrificed to belong. She was finally getting the respect she deserved. But it had come after years of scrutiny and criticism.

"So, your mother wanted you to come here."

Holly's laughter erupted. "Good heavens, no." She

took another sip of beer and composed herself. "It was Gran's idea. She was determined that I should know and appreciate my American roots. A friend of hers came to the island one summer, told her how wonderfully secluded it was. She rented the cottage under an alias and set the plans in motion. Her objective was that I would have as normal a childhood as could be had under the circumstances."

"Hard to fault her for that."

"My mother did," Holly replied dryly. "Believe me, it was a regular argument between the two of them."

"A battle royale?"

She sent him a black look.

"Sorry." He sipped his own beer. "So, what about your father? What did he think of your summers abroad?"

Her father? King Franco was a busy man. Sometimes she wondered if he remembered he had a daughter. She'd long felt like a disappointment.

"My father didn't think them necessary. After all, being royal is all he's ever known. But he didn't really care one way or another." She swallowed, determined to keep her tone nonchalant. "My being born female was a bit of a letdown, especially since he and my mother had no other children."

"But you're still the heir to the throne, right?"

"Yes."

"So?"

Holly shrugged. "He wanted a son." A fact that had caused Olivia no small amount of anxiety and dismay.

Her mother had already felt her new country found her lacking. When she failed to produce a male heir, well…

"I'm glad he didn't get his way."

Her cheeks grew warm. Even the storm's fury faded into the background as they eyed one another. Nate lifted a hand, stroked her cheek with his knuckles. The touch was light and brief. Her body's response was neither. And that was before his head tipped down and his lips brushed hers.

They'd kissed before. Her last summer on the island. A lifetime ago. The moment remained enshrined in her memory. It had been her first real kiss. Afterward, her heart had hammered and her breath had hitched.

"I love you."

The words had slipped out, soft and almost inaudible. But Nate had gathered her close and kissed her again, this time with more urgency. Even so, that long-ago kiss was nothing like this one, even if it held much of the same desperate yearning.

She'd never known this kind of need. It was every bit as brash and demanding as the storm battering the island. As such, it refused to be denied. She wound her arms tighter around Nate's neck, pulling their bodies together and giving in to the kind of passion that she'd only glimpsed in the past, and never with anyone but this man.

"Holly." Nate murmured her name.

His use of her nickname was enough to snap her back to the present. As much as she might wish things could be different, she was no longer an idealistic girl. She understood the futility of "if only," and so she ended things before they could progress too far.

Afterward, Nate pressed the cold base of his beer bottle against his forehead and closed his eyes.

"Some things get better with age," it sounded like he murmured.

She touched her lips. Indeed, they did.

"I wrote you a letter the first summer I didn't come. I wanted to explain why I wouldn't be here."

He lowered his hand, opened his eyes. "I never got a letter."

"That's because I didn't send it." It was folded up and tucked in her bureau drawer along with the other mementos of their summers together. Seashells, a picture of the first fish she'd caught, an old-fashioned glass cola bottle they'd found during a hike on the beach.

"Why?"

Because I was a coward. Because I was heartbroken. She sipped her beer, took her time swallowing.

"Because I didn't think you would understand."

"What I didn't understand was how you could just not return. Or write back. You never wrote back, Holly."

Guilt nipped hard as she recalled the letters Nate had written to her in care of the post office box her grandmother had set up. Gran had forwarded the letters faithfully, and Holly had read every one, her heart breaking anew when they'd finally stopped coming, although that was exactly what she'd expected to happen. What she told herself she wanted. Nate needed to move on with his life. Just as she was moving on with hers.

Hank snuffled loudly on the couch. Where the thunder hadn't roused him, the sound of his own snoring apparently did the trick. His eyelids flickered and he pulled himself to a sitting position, then scrubbed his face and offered a sheepish smile.

"Guess I drifted off." His gaze darted between the two of them. "Did I miss anything?"

"Just one hell of a storm," Nate said evenly before heading into the kitchen.

Holly waited until the weather settled down to call her parents. She had been gone nearly eighteen hours. Her father would be irritated by her disappearance. Her mother would be livid. A small part of her hoped they would also be worried. Instantly, she felt guilty. Of course, she didn't want them to worry. Besides, she was a grown woman. Wanting them to worry was childish, petty.

She sat on the edge of the bed and pulled out her cell phone. While she'd been in the shower, Nate must have been in her room. The window had been closed and the bed remade with fresh linens. A pale lavender coverlet was turned down, revealing floral sheets beneath. Leftovers from his parents, no doubt. The other ones would have been perfectly fine, but she appreciated his thoughtfulness. If only she could be sure it was thoughtfulness. Recalling the conversation she'd overheard earlier, she wondered if hospitality had been at the root of his actions, or embarrassment.

She's out of my league.

Long ago, Holly had come to terms with the fact that to some people—most people—she would always have a title before her name. Ultimately, that was why she hadn't been completely truthful with Nate when they were children.

When she'd started coming to the island at ten, her being a princess had been an afterthought in her mind. He was the son of northern Michigan resort owners. She was the daughter of European royalty. Later, she'd liked just a little too much that he saw her as a girl rather than, well, a goal. Even back then, the mothers of sons from around the kingdom had been busy trying to arrange meetings.

As if she hadn't felt conspicuous enough.

"Winning your favor would be quite a coup," Olivia had explained, when Holly had asked her mother about the fuss.

For the mothers or for the boys? she'd wondered. But Holly hadn't bothered to ask.

She frowned now. Not at the memories of awkward first dances and dinners, but at her phone. She wasn't getting a signal.

She was halfway down the stairs when Nate started up. They hadn't finished their earlier conversation; instead she'd taken the easy way out and retreated upstairs after Hank's untimely interruption.

They eyed one another warily now.

"Need something?" Nate asked.

"I was hoping to place a call to my parents, but my cell isn't receiving a signal."

"Only a couple of carriers work on the island and even then, service is spotty at best. You can use the phone in the kitchen," he offered.

It was on the tip of her tongue to remind him she would be phoning abroad and certain charges would apply. But since she'd already offended him once by offering to pay for her room, she remained mum. Somehow, she would find a way to compensate him.

"Thank you."

He nodded and started up. Two steps past her he stopped. "Do your parents know where you are?"

"Not exactly." The note she'd had Henry give Olivia just said that Holly was safe and would be in touch with contact information.

"Does anyone?"

She offered a half smile. "You do."

He frowned. "This island is a good place to get away, Holly, but people here read newspapers and own televisions. We're not backward."

"I never said you were," she replied defensively.

"But you thought it."

She folded her arms. "You don't know what I think."

"You're right. Sorry." The apology turned empty when he said, "I don't know you well enough."

She swallowed, a little unnerved by how badly it hurt for him to say so. There was a time when she'd thought he was the only person on the planet who remotely got who she was.

Nate continued. "Look, all I'm saying is that even Hank thought you looked familiar and he's hardly the sort to pay attention to the news, much less the tabloids."

She lifted her chin a notch. "As you said earlier, I managed to hide in plain sight when I was a girl."

"Yeah, but as *you* said earlier, you were decked out in shorts and pigtails back then."

"I left my tiara home for this trip, too," she said dryly. "And I didn't pack a single ball gown. I think I can fit in. Before the flight over with Hank, a woman in town told me I looked like Princess Hollyn. We both laughed. After all, what would Princess Hollyn Saldani of Morenci be doing here?"

"It's not the French Riviera," he agreed on a drawl.

"No. It's far more appealing."

Her satisfaction at his surprise was short-lived.

"Never been there, so I wouldn't know." With a shrug, he continued up the steps.

CHAPTER FOUR

"Where in God's name are you?" Olivia boomed as soon as she came on the line, her tone far more threatening than the earlier thunder.

Just as Holly had suspected, it wasn't worry that had her mother's voice rising a couple of octaves, but outrage. Holly brought the receiver back to her ear and replied, "I'm safe."

"That's not an answer, Hollyn."

"And I'm not a child, Mother."

"Then stop acting like one and return home immediately. You have obligations. You have functions to attend, some of which we have already had to postpone or cancel."

"I'm sorry."

Her mother's tone moderated and lost the Texas twang it acquired whenever Olivia was good and upset. "When can we expect you?"

"As I said in my note, I won't be gone long. I'll be home in a week." Holly wasn't sure what made her add, "Or closer to ten days."

"Hollyn!"

She held the phone away from her ear again, missing part of what her mother was saying. What she caught when she brought it back was "People are depending on you."

Holly's shoulders sagged even as her chest grew tight. "I know they are, Mother."

"I might have expected a stunt like this when you were in your teens, but you're a grown woman. I know it's different, but when I was your age, I was already wearing the Miss Texas crown and had competed nationally. I was living up to my obligations."

Vastly different, and that was your choice. But Holly didn't say the words out loud. She had no desire to rehash what was a very old argument and one she apparently had no hope of ever winning. In addition to knowing best, her mother was always right.

"Where are you?" Olivia asked a second time. "I'm assuming that you are no longer in Morenci. We've already checked all of your usual haunts and hideouts. Discreetly, of course, since the photographers have been on the lookout for you as well."

"Actually, I'm no longer in Europe. I'm in America."

"Heart Island."

Holly was sure her mother issued the words through clenched teeth.

"Yes."

"Why in God's name would you go there?"

Olivia had never understood either Gran's or Holly's attachment to the island. There was nothing to do on that rugged patch of land, she claimed. No department stores to shop at, no fancy restaurants to dine in, no culture whatsoever to be had unless one went to what remained of a British fort, one of the last holdings from the War of 1812. The fort itself had burned to the ground, but some of its foundation remained, and a large, green historical marker rose in the center, explaining the place's significance.

Big whoop, to use Olivia's old vernacular.

"It's peaceful here," Holly said. Even as the storm rumbled in the distance, she knew that to be true.

"It's peaceful at that discreet little spa that's tucked up in the hillside just outside Cannes."

Another argument that Holly couldn't win. Her and Olivia's views on what constituted a relaxing sojourn were just too different, which explained why her mother had been bored to tears the couple of times during Olivia's childhood that Gran had taken her camping. Fishing, beachcombing, hiking trails—those things had amounted to torture in Olivia's book.

As Gran used to say, "I guess my love for the outdoors skipped a generation."

And Olivia's love for wearing fancy gowns and a crown had skipped a generation, too.

"Phillip has called several times already," her mother said now.

Holly wanted to feel elated at the news or at least suitably guilty that the man she'd been linked with for the past several months was anxious to reach her. What she felt was…nothing. There was a great black hole in her emotions where Phillip was concerned.

They'd met more than a year ago when his company had been awarded one of the kingdom's highest honors for its environmental record. Her mother had insisted Holly call him personally after the award ceremony to invite him to the special dinner for honorees held at the palace.

She'd done so, and she'd sat next to him in the palace's opulent dining hall. They'd talked, laughed. It had been enough to convince Olivia of their suitability, especially given his flush bank account and impeccable breeding.

After that, Phillip had turned up at all sorts of events at the queen's urging. Holly was used to her mother's machinations. She'd seen no harm at first, despite Olivia's claim that it was time Holly settle down and marry.

"You'll be thirty before you know it." That warning first came not long after Holly turned twenty. These days it was her mother's stock phrase.

Phillip was handsome, thoughtful and accomplished. He treated Holly like the queen she would someday become. Both in public and in private he said all of the right things. He did all of the right things, too, deferring to her position, all while making it clear he was in no way without authority.

Yet, if he never called her again, Holly would easily forget he existed. That wasn't right, but it was a fact. One that only she seemed to think mattered. Even Phillip had changed the subject the few times she'd tried to broach it with him.

"You had plans to attend the opera for the opening night of *Madame Butterfly* last evening," her mother was reminding her. "His family box remained dark. We issued a press release saying you'd fallen ill, which also helped to explain your earlier absence from the annual garden show, but you know how easily rumors get started and then spread, Hollyn. I'm sure they are already swirling."

"Yes." And her mother was only too happy to help them along when it suited her agenda. Hence the widespread notion that an engagement to Phillip was imminent, even though Holly had been dragging her feet in accepting his proposal of marriage. "I'll call him later. Apologize."

Holly would, too. Phillip was a decent man. He deserved that much.

"He's worried about you. And a little hurt."

Holly felt a twinge of guilt. No matter her feelings—or lack of them—where Phillip was concerned, she hadn't intended to make him worry or hurt his feelings. "Phillip said that?"

"Well, not in so many words," her mother replied. "But I could hear it in his voice. You took off without a word to anyone, including him."

"Did you tell him the truth? Or does he also think I'm unwell."

"I thought it best to tell him the truth, just in case your image winds up in the tabloids, completely refuting our claims of illness. After all, the two of you are betrothed."

Holly's guilt evaporated. Annoyance took its place. "Phillip and I aren't betrothed. Yes, he's asked, but I haven't said yes, Mother."

A moot point, apparently. This was yet another decision being made by forces beyond Holly's control. Olivia's next words made that much clear.

"But you will. He's perfect for you, Hollyn. So much more pragmatic than you are, my dear," she said on a sigh. "That's exactly what you need. He'll help keep your feet planted firmly on the ground. Together, the two of you make an excellent team."

A team?

How lovely. And how romantic. But to her mother's way of thinking, when it came to the marriage of her only daughter, true love wasn't as important as blood-lines and tradition.

Olivia had her reasons, and Holly understood them even if she wasn't quite willing to bow to them any longer. Her parents' romance had been scandalous and deemed unacceptable by the older guard, including Holly's father's parents. Even though both of them were deceased now, Olivia was still desperate to toe the line and make her daughter do the same.

It had taken Olivia years to be taken seriously. For that reason, she was determined that her only child be above reproach.

Her mother continued. "Just as importantly, Phillip is the ideal husband for Morenci's future queen." Olivia ticked off his attributes, all of which Holly had heard before. "He comes from a prominent and well-regarded family. He has his own fortune, which grows daily thanks to his business acumen. If there are skeletons in the man's closet, none have been found. And believe me, your father and I have hired the most tenacious people to look."

"Mother—"

"I want to spare you the scrutiny your father faced for marrying me."

"You're a wonderful queen and a caring mother." It was true. Even as Holly chafed against Olivia's sometimes overbearing actions, she understood it was love that guided them.

"A spring wedding would be lovely," Olivia was saying. "It would give Morencians something to look forward to. And, God knows, with the current economic conditions and that nasty flood that damaged so much of the business district last fall, they need something to buoy their spirits. Your nuptials, my dear, are just what the doctor ordered for our country."

Forget the weight on her shoulders. Now, Holly felt queasy, and her legs turned to rubber. Before they gave out completely, she managed to slip onto one of the chairs at the kitchen table. Outside, the rain that an hour ago had been torrential was merely insistent as it tapped at the window.

She rubbed her left temple, feeling the beginnings of a headache start to take hold. So much responsibility, Holly thought, as the heavy yoke began to settle firmly into place once again.

"Mother, please."

"Fine. I'll leave talk of weddings to a later date. When can we expect you?"

"I already told you—"

"When?" Olivia interrupted.

A cartoon stuck to Nate's refrigerator door caught Holly's attention. It showed a sloe-eyed man lounging on a dock with a pole in one hand, a beverage in the other. Gone Fishing, it read. So simple. So utterly ideal. "A week at the earliest. I'll call if I decide to be longer."

"H-H-Hollyn!" Olivia sputtered.

Holly talked over her protest. "Sorry. I have to go.

There's a storm here and the reception isn't very good. I'll call again soon. I promise. Give my love to Father." And with that, she hung up.

Nate spied Holly when he reached the bottom of the stairs. She was seated on the couch with her arms wrapped around her knees, which she'd pulled to her chest. Her gaze was on the window, but he doubted she was seeing anything, both because of the darkness and the vacancy of her expression. Even a far-off flash of lightning failed to make her blink.

He almost turned back around. He didn't want to disturb her. But she looked so lost, and, given her pose and the way she'd pulled back her hair, a lot like the girl she'd been.

"I'm thinking that phone call didn't go very well."

She started at the sound of his voice and uncoiled. It was almost comical the way she smoothed down her shorts once her feet were settled on the ground, as if she were wearing a silk ball gown rather than simple cotton.

"Not very well, no."

"Parents worry," he said, thinking of his own. "I talk to my folks regularly and without fail my mother still asks if I've been taking my vitamins."

He'd hoped to get a laugh out of her, or at least a smile. Her frown deepened. "My relationship with my parents, my mother in particular, is a little more complicated."

"I know." He took a seat on the couch, leaving a full cushion between them.

"Sometimes I feel like she's more worried about how

I'll fare in the history books a few generations from now than, well, about me. I know she has her reasons, but…" Her frown deepened. "Let's talk about something else."

"Okay. What?"

She turned, the beginnings of a smile turning up the corners of her mouth. "How about you? From what you said earlier, I know you attended university and after graduation lived in Chicago for a time. What else?"

That was broad enough to keep him talking for hours. Nate would much rather rehash her life. God knew, he wanted some of the blanks filled in, blanks that the tabloids couldn't possibly know or get right. Had she really been in love with him all those years ago? Had she hoped, as much as he had, that they could find a way to be together? Did she love this guy she was supposedly going to marry?

Instead of asking any of those questions, he nodded.

He wasn't completely comfortable talking about himself, especially since his life, even what he considered the highlights, might not be all that exciting from her point of view. But she smiled, nodded encouragingly, as he told her about the summer internship he'd had between his junior and senior years of college at a hotel in New York's Times Square.

"New York is something," Holly said. "So much energy and so much to do. It's my mother's favorite city, though she wouldn't admit to that publicly for obvious reasons."

"It's something," he agreed. Though he had a feeling she'd enjoyed a bird's-eye view from some penthouse apartment, where he'd shared a tiny walk-up with four other interns in a section of the city that wouldn't make it on any tourist maps.

"Anyway, after graduation from the University of Michigan, I took a job in Chicago and attended Northwestern in the evenings to earn my MBA."

"I'm impressed."

He shrugged, but damn if he wasn't warmed by her compliment.

"And now I'm here."

"Doing what you love."

She'd summed it up perfectly. All he could do was nod.

"I envy you that," she said softly.

"You envy me." He realized as soon as he said it that he'd insulted her.

"My apologies. I forgot. I have the world by its tail. I have no cares, no concerns, no worries whatsoever beyond which silver spoon to select to eat my next meal. I'm not allowed to envy anyone anything."

She started to rise to her feet. Nate put a hand on her arm to stop her. "I didn't mean—"

She closed her eyes and exhaled slowly, as if reaching deep inside herself for patience. Apparently, she found it. When she opened her eyes, she looked calm and only the slightest bit weary. She straightened her shoulders, tilted her chin up. She was the polar opposite of the woman he'd come across mere minutes ago, legs pulled to her chest and lost in thought.

If Nate had to pick one word to describe her it would be *regal*. And he meant it as a compliment, even if he also knew what it was costing her. *I'm always on dis-*

play, she'd said earlier. Which meant she knew how to play the part of princess.

"Of course you didn't. It's all right. I'm tired and being insufferably rude, especially after all you've done for me."

He'd offered her a place to stay for the night—a little begrudgingly at first—showed her how to operate the ancient shower in the guest bath, shared a beer and allowed her the use of his phone. He'd hardly been put out. He said as much.

"But I do appreciate it, especially since my visit was so unexpected."

Nate rose to his feet. He felt like a champion heel. Holly was apologizing, but he was the one who was sorry. Not only for the thoughtless comment he'd made, but also for the effect his words had had on her mood. It was as if a light had been doused. He didn't like knowing he'd done the dousing.

"It's no problem, you being here. If I've seemed, well, a little brusque, it's just that I'm not good with surprises," he said. "I like to know what's coming next."

"I'd rather enjoy a few surprises now and again. Part of the problem for me is I know exactly what to expect. The script has been written. I'm just acting out the scenes."

He'd never thought of it that way.

"I think I'll retire now."

"It's been a long day," he agreed.

"Yes. Very."

He waited until she was at the base of the steps to turn out the lamp. Enough light spilled from the open door of his bedroom at the top of the stairs to keep them from tripping.

It was odd, walking up to his bedroom with a beautiful woman at his side and knowing they would part ways at the top of the steps and nothing would happen but sleep. Or sleeplessness, as the case likely would be for him.

He'd entertained overnight guests of the opposite sex before. He was a grown man, after all. And he'd hardly lived as a monk.

But this was different. This was something…more. He might not like it, but that was a fact. He'd accepted that earlier when they'd kissed. The mere memory of it would haunt him, just as memories of a suntanned teenage girl had haunted him for the past decade, whether he'd wanted to admit it or not.

At the top of the steps, she turned, as he'd known she would, starting to the opposite end of the house after offering a polite smile and the appropriate good-night wish. Words stuck in Nate's throat, jumbled up on his tongue.

I'm glad you're here. He nearly said it. And he *was* glad. In spite of everything and all of the conflicting emotions seeing her again had prompted, he was.

But instead of telling her so, he stepped into his bedroom and closed the door. After stripping off his shirt and shorts, he stretched out on the cool cotton sheets, eyeing the shadows cast from the lamp on the nightstand, as his mind tried to make sense of his thoughts.

He'd gotten over Holly. A long time ago, in fact. It hadn't been easy those first couple of summers, but then he'd gone off to college, dated other girls both on the island and elsewhere. Even if none of those relationships had lasted long or held any deep meaning for him, it wasn't as if he'd been pining. He'd figured the feelings he'd had for Holly had only felt so intense because he'd been young and in love for the first time.

That had made sense.

Now, here she was again. Back on the island after all of these years. She'd been in his life for mere hours, already upsetting its careful balance in ways he couldn't begin to fathom. And while Nate wished he could say that he'd been right, that immaturity and imagination had been responsible for those inflated feelings of the past, he knew he would be lying.

She was special.

Nate the boy had loved Holly the girl. After the kiss of a couple hours ago, he knew that Nate the man could very well wind up in a similar predicament.

If he allowed it.

He didn't plan to allow it. After all, just like before, she would be leaving. In mere days, she would go back to a life that Nate wasn't part of and never could be.

No, he wouldn't make the mistake of falling in love with Holly twice.

CHAPTER FIVE

NATE awoke just before dawn, not that he'd slept much knowing that Holly was just down the hall, stretched out between the sheets he'd spread over his boyhood bed.

Oh, the irony, given the many fantasies he'd entertained of her there back when they both were teenagers, when his hormones had been churning on high.

Between her nearness and Hank's buzz-saw snoring, Nate barely had managed a few hours of shut-eye. Add to that his anxiety over the extent of the storm's damage to the resort, and it was no wonder he was suffering insomnia. At first light, he dressed and prepared to head out.

Hank was still sleeping. The noise coming from the other man's room confirmed as much. Nate glanced down the hall. Before he could stop himself, he was at Holly's door. He leaned in close and listened. The only sound he could hear was breathing and it was coming from him. She was probably dead to the world, a casualty of jet lag. He started to step away, then stopped. Even though it made absolutely no sense, and he knew he was being unforgivably rude, he slowly turned the knob, pushed the door open a crack and peeked inside.

Just as he'd suspected, Holly was asleep. She was

on her side, facing him. She looked lovely, if troubled. Even in sleep her brow appeared furrowed. She'd come to the island to get away. Even as he wanted to believe it wasn't his business or his concern, he couldn't help wondering, from what exactly? She'd mentioned how scripted her life was. But she was a princess, high enough up the royal food chain that surely she could call some of the shots. So what exactly was she running from?

Or whom?

That guy she was linked to? Nate's hands fisted at the thought.

She sighed then, turned. Honey-colored hair spilled over the pillow. His pillow.

Lucky pillow.

A sound rose in his throat—part moan, part curse. Nate closed the door with a smart click and hurried downstairs. Mere minutes later, armed with a Thermos full of black coffee and a clipboard, he hopped in his pickup truck.

He spent the first hour riding from one end of the resort to the other, jotting down notes and prioritizing the cleanup as he went. This was how he approached problems: head-on and with a plan. Doing so was not only practical, but in this instance it also helped keep his mind off of Holly.

As he drove, a calm settled over him, despite the obvious fallout from the storm. This was his kingdom. Last night, he'd experienced some doubts. They'd cleared off with the storm. He'd made the right choices in his life. This was where he wanted to be. The resort was a grand enough dream for him. He was happy here. The island was home.

He'd already called in the Burns twins to help. The boys were seventeen, with strong backs and a deep desire to earn enough cash to buy their first car. Their dream vehicle was a vintage restored Mustang the island's only doctor had put up for sale. So they were only too happy to hear Nate had extra hours for them to work.

As he drove, Nate stopped to chat with any guests who were out and about. Several of them were, especially those who had come to the island to fish.

"That was quite the storm last night," Ernie Smithe commented. "Reminded me of the one back in eighty-seven."

The older man haled from a suburb just outside of Detroit and had been coming north for two weeks in June for as long as Nate could remember. He was seated at the picnic table just outside his cabin, a steaming cup of coffee at his elbow as he went through his tackle box.

"Yes, it was." Nate nodded at the selection of lures. "What are you fishing for this morning?"

"Anything that will take the bait." The older man laughed then. "I haven't had too much luck trolling off the little islands just outside the bay."

"Perch are biting off the marina's dock. Your best bet is minnows." Nate sold them for a couple dollars per dozen in the shop. "Tell the kid working the counter that I said to give you a complimentary bucketful."

The way Nate saw it, it was a small price to pay for the fact the storm had taken out the resort's cable television. He made a note to himself to tell anyone who worked the desk that minnows were on the house for the rest of the day.

Ernie thanked him. Nate started on his way. As he passed his cottage, he thought he saw movement through the kitchen window. He pulled the truck to a stop and headed up the steps, bracing himself a moment before pulling open the door. He wasn't sure what to say. *Good morning* would be appropriate. But for some reason asking if she'd slept well seemed a little too personal.

Then again, that kiss had been nothing if not personal.

He scrubbed a hand over his face at the memory, felt the stubble. He hardly looked his best. He didn't want to care. But he did. God help him. He did.

It turned out there was no need for divine intervention. The person standing in his kitchen was Hank. The other man was hunched over the counter helping himself to a bowl of cold cereal.

"Mornin'," he mumbled around a mouthful of fortified flakes.

"Hey." Nate glanced past him. The television was on but the living room was empty.

"She's not up yet," Hank said, doing a lousy job of hiding his amusement.

Nate ignored him. "I checked on your plane."

That got his attention. "How'd she fare?"

"No worse for the wear. Good thing we beached and tethered her, though. A couple of the boats that were moored in the shallows got tossed about quite a bit. One is going to need a new prop."

"Good thing," Hank repeated, his complexion a little pale. He set the now-empty bowl in the sink. "And thanks for the place to stay last night. You're not a bad host, Matthews, even if we never did get around to that poker game."

Nate laughed. "No problem."

Hank hitched a thumb over his shoulder in the direction of the stairs. "So, what are you going to do about your other guest?"

"What do you mean?"

"The lady needs a place to stay," Hank reminded him. As if Nate needed reminding on that score.

"I'll find her something on the island."

"Sure about that?" Hank scratched his scruffy chin. He had a good decade on Nate. Right now, he was acting as if he were his father. "You said last night most places were full up. Kind of scolded the girl, as I recall, for coming without advance notice."

"I'm sure there's something she can rent." Especially given Holly's unlimited budget. With that kind of cash to flash around, even the exclusive private summer residences that dotted the bay's eastern shore would likely be open to renters. Since Hank seemed to be waiting for greater reassurance, Nate added, "I'll drive her around later, see what's available."

"As long as you're sure she won't wind up down at the campground."

"The campground." Nate snorted out a laugh. The Holly he'd known as a child would have been fine in a pup tent, roasting marshmallows over an open fire and swapping ghost stories. They'd done just that her second summer on the island. In separate tents pitched outside the cottage her grandmother rented. This Holly? She would be carried off by the mosquitoes that sometimes were mistaken for Michigan's state bird.

He laid a hand over his heart. "I promise, I won't allow her to wind up at the campground."

"Okay." Hank nodded. "I'll be heading out in a bit. I've got a couple fares scheduled for later this morning. You tell her she can call me if need be. I'll come back for her in a flash."

"I'm sure she won't be needing your services."

"Just see that you tell her." The other man was all business now. Nate would have found Hank's edict annoying if he didn't also appreciate that he was looking out for Holly.

That made two of them.

"I will."

Holly woke to the far-off squawk of seagulls, the sound of gently lapping waves and the smell of freshly brewed coffee. The storm was long gone, and from the sunshine peeking through the curtains, it was but a distant memory at this point.

She stretched on the mattress and smiled sleepily as she regarded the outdated, overhead light fixture. Overall, she'd slept well, deep and dreamless. It was peaceful here, and so quiet.

She amended her opinion a moment later when the jarring roar of a chainsaw had her lurching out of bed. A peek out one of the windows and she found its source. Nate was just down the beach from the cottage, holding the offending power tool in his hands and using it to slice through the thick trunk of a fallen cedar tree.

She noted other trees and branches strewn about

the beach and wondered what the full impact of the
storm had been on the resort. She glanced around. Hank
wasn't with him. Nor was the pilot's seaplane visible on
the beach. But Nate did have a couple of helpers, teenage boys unless Holly missed her guess. And from the
looks of it, they were as impressed with his skill with
the chainsaw as she was.

She decided to get dressed after a glance at the clock
on the nightstand revealed it was closing in on noon.
Noon! By her calculations, she'd slept nearly a dozen
hours. How on earth had she managed to sleep that
long? Sure, she was jet-lagged. But back home she rou-
tinely ran on four to five hours of sleep a night, and even
that, lately, had been punctuated with bouts of wakeful-
ness.

Dressed in a pair of white capris, a crisp cotton
blouse the color of raspberries and the burnished silver gladiator sandals that she'd picked up after attend-
ing a fashion show in Milan, she headed downstairs.
As she'd already determined, Hank was nowhere to be
found. He'd probably flown to the mainland hours ago,
which meant she had no way back. At least not right
now. Which meant she was at Nate's mercy. She wasn't
sure how she felt about that.

In the kitchen, there was exactly one cup of coffee
left in the maker. Though she preferred tea, she didn't
feel like rooting around in Nate's cupboards to see if
he had any. She poured the coffee for herself, shut off
the pot and instantly felt guilty. Americans liked their
coffee, or so her mother claimed. Nearly thirty years
in Morenci and Olivia still eschewed tea in favor of a
nice cup of Colombian. She could drink a pot by her-

self, all while complaining about the effects of caffeine on one's body and complexion.

Holly decided to make a second pot. She would bring a cup out to Nate. It would be a peace offering of sorts.... A thank-you, she amended. She eyed the maker dubiously. As enamoured as she was with prospect of cooking, she didn't have much skill in the kitchen. *Much* as in next to none. Anytime she attempted something remotely culinary her mother would remind her they had "staff" to deal with that.

Thus, Holly also had little experience when it came to small appliances, and this looked nothing like the ones she'd glimpsed in the palace kitchens. Still, it seemed simple enough. Besides, the brewing instructions were listed on the inside of the lid that opened where she had to add the water. How hard could it be? Only an idiot could screw it up.

It turned out Holly was an idiot.

One look at Nate's face after he took the first sip and she knew it for a fact.

God bless him, the man managed to swallow what he had in his mouth rather than spit it out in sprinkler fashion. But his grimace spoke volumes.

"That's...a little strong," he said after a moment.

"I followed the directions," she countered as the identical-looking young men standing on either side of Nate studied their sneakers.

"Let me guess. You used the scoop in the coffee jar as your measure."

"Of course I did."

"It's double the amount."

"How was I supposed...?" She let the question trail

off and crossed her arms over her chest instead. "Real men like it strong."

Nate blinked at that. The teens eyed one another, their expressions all but asking, "Did she really just say that?" From what Holly knew of the American teenage boy's vernacular, she added, "Dude."

"I like my coffee strong," Nate said in seeming agreement.

"Good."

"I just prefer to have my stomach lining left intact afterward."

Delivered as it was in that even pitch of his, with the beginnings of a smile turning up the corners of his lips, it was hard to take offense. Impossible, in fact. Holly dissolved into giggles. The boys joined in her laughter, too, but only once Nate had let out a snort of amusement. As one who appreciated loyalty, she instantly liked them.

"Sorry," she said at last. "Truly, I wasn't trying to poison you."

"It's okay." He tossed the rest of the coffee to the ground and handed back the cup. "I appreciate the effort."

Whether intended as a peace offering or as a thank-you, the coffee seemed to do the trick. Some of the old ease they'd had with one another returned.

Nate seemed to remember his manners. "Josh and Joey Burns, this is…Holly. She used to come to the island a lot as a kid. She's back now for a short visit."

She refused to acknowledge the way her heart sank at his description of her visit as being short. What else could it be? It wasn't as if she could stay on Heart indefinitely. She couldn't just quit being a princess and relocate to a foreign country. Could she?

"Holly?" Nate prompted.

"Sorry. My mind wandered." Wandered? It had taken a trip into uncharted territory. She pasted on a smile. "It's nice to meet you both."

"Hi," each of the boys said, looking a little shy and adorably awkward as they accepted her outstretched hand.

"You talk funny," Josh—or was it Joey?—said. His cheeks turned blotchy immediately after saying so. "I don't mean funny, more like, you know, different. You have an accent of some sort."

"Smooth," his brother muttered half under his breath.

"I'm not from your country," Holly said. She couldn't help thinking they had a bit of an accent, too. American English definitely carried a different sound than British English, which she was far more used to.

The other brother spoke up then. "Has anyone ever told you that you look like someone famous?"

Holly and Nate traded glances.

"No. Whom do you mean?" she asked, keeping her expression carefully blank. This was exactly what Nate had warned her would happen, and what she wanted to avoid.

"Lady Gaga."

"What?" Holly let out a completely unladylike snort of laughter that would have earned her mother's censure. As it was, it had Nate's eyebrows rising. "I can honestly say that no one has ever told me I look like the pop star."

"Not when she's done all up for, like, a concert or an

awards show or anything," Josh was quick to correct. "She can be pretty out there. But you kind of have the same eyes."

"Really." More amused than incredulous now, Holly sent a grin in Nate's direction. "Lady Gaga. What do you think?"

He shook his head. "Sorry. I'm not seeing it."

She turned back to the twins. "Don't feel bad. Nate is more of a country-Western sort. Or at least he was back when we were children."

Garth Brooks, George Strait, Alan Jackson and a little Brooks & Dunn had been staples on his stereo. He'd known the songs by heart. He'd even taught Holly to two-step. The first time she'd gotten the movements right without his prompting, he'd swung her around in a circle and kissed her cheek before setting her down and quickly stepping away. They'd been on his parents' deck. She'd been fourteen. He'd been…her world.

"I've grown into a heavy metal fan since then," he informed her now.

Holly's mouth gaped open a moment before she could say, "You did not."

He merely shrugged. "My college roommate was a huge AC/DC fan. It was either learn to like screeching lyrics and wicked electric guitar riffs or sleep at the library. I chose the path of least resistance and the most shut-eye. Besides, it's not so bad once you get used to it."

"'Back in Black.'" One of the boys nodded and grinned. "Totally."

"Totally," the other one echoed.

"Righteous," Holly said, flipping what she thought

was the sign she'd seen rock stars use, but earning confused glances from all three of the males in her presence. She could only hope the sign she'd flashed hadn't been offensive.

"Start loading these logs into the pickup," Nate instructed.

The boys did as they were told. Holly asked in a lowered voice, "Did I get that wrong?"

"A finger or two. You gave us the Boy Scout salute." Nate started to chuckle.

"Oh." She picked a coffee ground out of the otherwise empty cup. "Heavy metal. I guess it makes sense that your tastes have changed since I was last here."

She tried to keep her tone light, but the way Nate was looking at her made it difficult.

"We were kids then."

"Children," she agreed.

His gaze skimmed down. Awareness simmered between them.

"Not all of my tastes have changed," he said.

"No?"

He glanced away. When his gaze returned to hers it was far more impassive. "I still like toasted marshmallows."

Nate told the Burns brothers to take a break for lunch and walked with Holly back to the house, intending to do the same. He was still a little surprised that she'd come out to find him, bringing with her a cup of coffee no less. The worst cup of coffee he'd ever had, but still. It was definitely the thought that counted.

"It looks like you have a lot of work to do," she

remarked, stepping over one of the many downed branches strewn over the resort grounds.

The beach had been cleared first and the sand freshly graded. Already, families were out, lounging in chairs and watching their children build sand castles or play in the water. This was exactly why it had been the priority. When people came to an island, they expected unfettered access to the water.

"Enough. But it's not as bad as I feared it would be." He gave her a quick summary of what his morning tour had turned up. "Besides, the twins will help. They're good kids. Strong backs and a burning desire to make a buck. They have their eye on a car. A real babe magnet."

Holly's brow crinkled.

"A stylish ride sure to turn all the young girls' heads," Nate translated.

"You drove a station wagon, as I recall," she said.

With the resort logo plastered on the doors. He grimaced. "That was the opposite of a babe magnet."

"And yet you managed to turn my head." She blushed after saying so and then changed the subject. "The twins seem nice."

Nate nodded. "Although maybe not all that bright." He gave her arm a poke. "They thought you looked like Lady Gaga."

"Yes." She shook her head. "I'm still trying to figure out if I should be flattered."

She batted the lashes on the eyes the boys claimed were like the pop star's. The gesture was silly, as silly as the boys' assertion. But Nate's mouth went dry as he stared at her. He'd always thought Holly's eyes were one of her best features.

"They're so damned blue," he murmured.

"Pardon me?"

Nate fiddled with the clipboard he'd snagged from the front seat of his truck. He'd brought it with him mostly to keep his hands occupied. Wouldn't it just figure that it was his mouth making him into a fool?

"Uh, Hank took off a couple hours ago."

"Yes. I noticed that his plane was gone when I left your house."

Of course she had.

"He had some fares, so he needed to return to the mainland."

It was a lie—little and white—since the pilot would have stuck around if Nate hadn't insisted that he would find Holly a place to stay.

"I guess this means I'm at your mercy." She blushed again.

Nate's heart did a funny little flip. Holly. At his mercy. He was guy enough that some serious fantasies could be attached to such a statement, benign though she'd intended it. He nearly pinched his thumb under the board's clip, and cleared his throat.

"After we eat lunch, I'll take you around to the other resorts as well as to the real estate office in town. Nadine Masterson runs it. She'll know if there is anything available to rent, even if it's not listed. Some of the more exclusive places aren't advertised."

"Thank you. I appreciate it."

Holly's smile was polite. And fake. It was the kind of smile she wore for public appearances. Since Nate was

privy to the real thing, he spotted the imposter easily
enough. Less than twenty-four hours in her presence
and he'd already figured out that retreating behind good
manners was a way for her to mask her true feelings.
She'd never done that as a girl. Back then, she'd given as
good as she'd gotten, arguing and opining like a champion debater. He'd been fascinated by her passion for
life and adventure and, later, for him, as innocent as it
had been.

Recalling that now, he asked, "Why do you do that?"

She blinked. "What do you mean?"

"You're saying one thing when it's clear you mean
another."

"I'm afraid I still don't know what you mean."

"You're smiling, saying how appreciative you are,
but I don't get the feeling you're very happy."

"Why wouldn't I be happy?" she argued. "As I said,
I appreciate the trouble you're going to, helping me find
a place to stay elsewhere on the island."

Nate thought he had his answer. She hadn't just come
to Heart Island. She'd come to the Haven Resort. "If I
had a cottage available, I'd rent it to you. I know I may
not have been very gracious when you first arrived last
night, but..."

She smiled—the real thing this time—and clasped
her hands in front of her. "I believe you would. Thank
you, Nate."

He hadn't done anything. Yet. But he would. He
would see to it that Holly found a place to stay on Heart
and that she enjoyed her time away from her royal duties.

Maybe along the way, she not only would remember

the girl she'd once been, she would find a little of that girl's spirit still within her.

They ate a simple lunch of grilled cheese sandwiches. Unfortunately, one look through his refrigerator and pantry and that was about all Nate could come up with.

He'd meant to get to the grocery store. He was even running low on staples such as milk, eggs and bread. Truth be told, Nate dined out more than he ate in. He liked the company to be found at the Fishing Hole, a pub on the other side of the bay that served the best deep-fried white fish on the island. Even if he came in alone, he never sat alone. Everyone knew everyone. The island was a community in the best sense of the word.

Holly didn't complain about the pedestrian fare. Not that Nate expected her to. He'd already figured out that she hadn't changed quite as much as he'd thought she had in terms of her tastes, and that, despite their earlier conversation, she would kill him with kindness rather than utter any intentionally rude comments.

He missed the young woman who had been full of opinions and dreams, which she'd shared without any prompting at all. One, he still remembered.

"I'm going to be an artist someday. So good, that you probably won't be able to afford my work."

The memory had him asking, "Do you still paint?"

She had a mouthful of grilled cheese. She stopped chewing, blinked a couple of times. It was a moment before she swallowed and could reply.

"I…no. Not much. There's really no time."

"I'm surprised." And he was. "I remember someone once telling me that a person makes time for the things that are important."

"I was never any good at it. It's not as if anything I painted was going to wind up hanging in a museum or for sale in a gallery."

"That doesn't mean it wasn't important."

"I...I..." Whatever she'd intended to say went unfinished. Instead, she stood, pushing back from the table so abruptly that her chair nearly tipped over. Her expression wasn't sad exactly. Nor did she appear angry. But it was clear she was upset.

"Hol—"

But she was already gone, her footsteps thudding on the carpeted steps.

Holly paced the length of her room, equal parts agitated and embarrassed. She'd acted like a fool, dashing out of the kitchen like that. But she couldn't stay, not when Nate saw her so clearly. She'd felt naked, exposed and ashamed. Ashamed of how she'd let her needs and desires be subjugated.

She'd loved painting, especially with watercolors. In each brushstroke she'd found respite from daily pressures. Yet she'd allowed herself to be steered away from being an artist and toward being a patron of the arts.

"I remember someone once telling me that a person makes time for the things that are important."

Yes, she'd said that. She'd believed it, too.

How had she allowed herself to forget?

CHAPTER SIX

As NATE suspected, pretty much every resort on the island was at capacity. Even a couple of the questionable places on the far side of the island were posting No Vacancy signs.

Holly had been awfully quiet throughout their drive. He'd made no mention of what had happened in the kitchen. It was clear she didn't want to talk about whatever it was that had prompted her hasty departure.

Beside him in the cab of his truck, he heard Holly sigh.

"It's not looking good, is it?" she said.

"No, but we'll swing by the real estate office. As I said, Nadine has resources that I don't."

"Maybe I should just call Hank to come get me."

"And what? Go home?"

She stared straight ahead. From the way her nose wrinkled, he was pretty sure she found the option distasteful, yet she said, "God knows, my mother would be relieved."

Would Nate be? Would he be relieved to have the status quo restored? It was a question he wasn't ready to answer. So, he reminded Holly, "You came here looking for something."

"Yes, I did." She plucked at the hem of her blouse. "Something that may no longer exist, and even if it does…"

"Yes?" he prodded.

"You not only have to make time for the things that are important, Nate, you have to have the courage to make that time."

It was an interesting answer. One that begged questions. But Nate didn't ask what she meant. She wasn't the only one lacking for nerve. "We'll go and talk to Nadine. There's plenty of time to call Hank later if nothing pans out."

"All right."

She leaned her head back on the rest. They were on one of the island's main roads. Every car that passed going in the opposite direction, the driver waved.

"People are so friendly here," she remarked.

"We all know one another, the locals, that is. And, even the tourists do it once they've been around for a while. When people wave, the natural reaction is to wave back."

"Like this?" She cupped her hand slightly and gave what he thought of as a royal wave. A smile turned up the corners of her mouth.

"That's a 'how do you do' sort of wave. Here on the island, we keep our fingers splayed a bit and use more wrist. It says, 'Hey. How's it going? Have a good one.'" Nate demonstrated.

"I see what you mean," Holly said in mock seriousness. They passed a pickup truck and she gave her best imitation.

"Now you're getting the hang of it."

They both laughed.

She turned and smiled. "Thank you, Nate."

"For teaching you how to give a proper Heart Island wave?"

"For making me laugh and, well, ferrying me about from place to place."

"It's nothing."

"It is," she disagreed. "I've taken you away from your work for a good portion of the day, and after a vicious storm no less. I'm sure you have better things to do with your time."

"Other things to do, maybe. But not better," he corrected on a smile.

He reached across the truck's bench seat and gave her hand a squeeze. He wanted to hold it, weave his fingers through hers and maybe stroke the soft skin he encountered with the pad of his thumb. Instead, he released her hand and gripped the steering wheel with both of his.

"To Heart Island Realty," he said.

The business in question was located near what the islanders referred to as the Four Corners. It was the main intersection just off the ferry landing on the island, and as such, the hub of commerce. Whether tourist or local, pretty much everyone converged on the Four Corners at one point or another during the week.

Stub's Grocery dominated one corner, a hardware and feed store another. The remaining two were taken up with Mary Sue's Mercantile, which sold men's, women's and children's clothing as well as home goods; and Dan's Laundromat, which both shared a parking lot with Phoebe's Frozen Treats. Just down from that, and in the same shared parking lot, was Heart Island Realty.

Nate pulled his truck into one of the available spots. Together, he and Holly entered the business.

Nadine Masterson glanced up when the cowbell over the door rang. She was a pretty woman, petite, with brown hair that she wore short these days. She was the same age as Nate. She and her younger sister had moved to the island when Nadine was a senior in high school. It had been quite an adjustment for both of the girls, even though they hadn't come from a large city. Even small cities had a broader social circle than the island did. Nate had asked Nadine to their senior prom. They'd dated on and off over the years, never seriously, but they enjoyed one another's company. Their nights out had become a little more frequent since his return to the island a few years earlier. Still, they were anything but exclusive and not in what he would consider a committed relationship.

He began to wonder if maybe she felt otherwise when her face split into a grin when she glanced up and saw him. The smile was a little more intimate than the one saved for a mere friend. The way Holly stiffened, Nate figured she'd picked up on that, too. He could have smacked himself upside the head for his lapse in judgment. Well, there was no help for it now.

"Nate Matthews," Nadine was saying as she came around the desk. "If you aren't a sight for sore eyes on a what has otherwise been a really lousy day."

"Hey, Nadine." He reached for Holly, who stood just behind him, and guided her forward. He immediately regretted the proprietary hand he'd rested on the small of Holly's back. Both women seemed to have a visceral reaction to the gesture.

Nadine's smile evaporated. Holly jumped.

"And who might this be?"

"This is—"

"I'm Holly. An old friend of Nate's family." She stepped to the side, just outside his reach, and extended a hand to the other woman.

"Nadine Masterson."

"It's nice to meet you, Ms. Masterson." Holly folded her hands in front of her. "I arrived on the island rather unexpectedly late yesterday. Unfortunately, Nate's resort is full, but he brought me to you in the hope that you might find something available for me elsewhere on the island."

How nonthreatening was that? Nate nearly felt insulted.

Nadine divided a gaze between the two of them. Nate could only imagine what she was thinking, and it was a good bet he would hear all about it the next time they ran into one another at the Fishing Hole.

He wouldn't have to wait that long, he decided, when Nadine said, "You arrived yesterday, Holly?"

"Yes, late. Hank Whitey flew me over from the mainland."

"Really. That was bold of him, considering the storm."

"It was before it hit."

"I see."

Two words that in Nate's experience were women-speak for anything but.

Holly didn't bat an eye. She remained the picture of

calm and contrition. "Hank and I wound up overnight guests at Nate's home."

"How convenient."

"Yes. They are both very kind men. But then, in Nate's case, given how far our families go back, I'm sure he felt obligated to look after me."

Nadine's brows rose at that. Her gaze cut to Nate for a moment before returning to Holly. "Just how far back do you go?"

"To childhood. In fact, I haven't seen Nate since we were mere children."

Okay, that was an exaggeration. It's not as if they'd been toddling about in diapers, but he decided not to correct her.

Holly said, "We lost touch over the years. I wasn't even aware that his parents had retired and were no longer in charge of the resort when I decided to come for a visit."

"Oh." Nadine's posture was no longer quite so rigid.

"Now, I'm hoping to get out of Nate's hair, I believe the saying is, and find a place to stay for the remainder of my trip."

"And how long might that be?"

"Ten days." In his peripheral vision, Nate saw Holly lick her lips before adding, "Or so."

Interesting. The duration of her visit kept lengthening. Equally interesting, he wasn't sure how he felt about that.

"Let me see what I can do." Nadine returned to her desk and booted up her computer. A few keystrokes later, she was frowning. "I hate to tell you this, but pretty much all of the private residences that rent out are booked at least through Sunday." It was Thursday. "After that, I can set you up in a nice chalet on the eastern tip of the bay."

"You'd be directly across the bay from the resort," Nate added.

"I thought that was all state or federally owned land?" Holly said.

At Nadine's questioning gaze, Nate said, "We used to hike it when we were kids." To Holly, he replied, "There are a few acres of private land along the coast."

"It's a little secluded as a result," Nadine added. "But it has a generous private beach and offers terrific views of Lake Huron. It also comes with the use of a couple of personal watercraft and a canoe. The owners live downstate. They're rarely here, so they rent it out. It's in high demand."

"I can see why. It sounds lovely."

Nadine sucked air in around her teeth. "Yes, well, its rental price reflects that."

She rattled off a sum that was three times more than the going rate of Nate's largest and most well-appointed cabin. He could only imagine what the inside of the chalet must look like as Nadine was telling Holly about a jetted tub in the master bath and granite countertops and a wine cooler in a gourmet kitchen. He'd gone by the outside in his fishing boat on several occasions. It certainly didn't lack for windows or outdoor living space with a deck that wrapped around the lower floor and a balcony off the upper one.

"The owners only rent by the week, so if you stay, say, ten days, you would still have to pay for the full two weeks."

"It will become available on Sunday?" Holly asked, clearly unaffected by the amount.

Nate saw Nadine's eyes widen slightly, as if she'd figured it would be too rich for Holly's blood. If only she knew. Still, she was all business.

Nadine folded her hands on the desk blotter. "Yes. That's when the current guests are scheduled to leave. Checkout is noon. You could check in by three o'clock, maybe even a little earlier depending on how much work housekeeping has to do."

"Thank you. I'll take it. For two weeks."

Nadine gaped and so did Nate, neither of them quite able to contain their surprise. One week had become ten days and now ten days had turned into two weeks. Two weeks that would start on Sunday.

"Don't you want to see it first?" Nadine asked.

"No. I'm sure it will be fine."

"All right." Nadine typed up the rental agreement. If she wondered at the Texas post office box Holly gave for an address, she never let it show. However, her eyes widened for a second time when Holly opened her handbag and paid the entire sum in traveler's checks.

Handing her the receipt, Nadine asked, "So, where will you be staying between now and Sunday?"

Though the question was tendered casually, there was nothing casual about it. And they all knew it.

"Somewhere on the mainland." Holly turned to Nate. "I'll need to call Hank when we get back to your house."

"Sure."

He turned and thanked Nadine.

"Will you be at the Fishing Hole tonight?" she asked.

"I, um…" His gaze cut to Holly. "Probably not. I've got a lot of work to catch up with at the resort."

Nadine nodded. Holly smiled politely. No one made direct eye contact. As they took their leave, Nate couldn't escape the feeling that he was in hot water with both women.

Holly was fuming, even though she told herself she had absolutely no right to her anger. Still, she felt like a fool, and that seemed reason enough to give it vent. She waited until they were in the truck, seat belts buckled, to say in as casual a tone as she could muster, "Your girlfriend is very pretty."

Nate cleared his throat as he stuck the key in the ignition. "Nadine is *not* my girlfriend."

"Oh?" Holly puckered her lips, unconvinced. "Does she feel the same way?"

The truck's engine revved to life, and he shifted into gear. He spared her a glance before he looked both ways for oncoming cars and then pulled out of the parking lot. The truck's tires squealed and spat gravel, and she figured she had her answer, even before Nate said, "Look, we date…sometimes. Okay?"

Why did hearing him say that make her heart hurt? And it did. There was a funny ache in the center of her chest. Which was ridiculous. She had no claim on Nate. Whatever had been between them had ended practically before it began, and that was a very, very long time ago.

Their kiss of the evening before flashed in her mind, every bit as impossible to ignore as the lightning that had flashed in the sky during it. With it, needs she hadn't known existed had filtered to the forefront.

"You might have mentioned it." The words slipped from her lips before she could stop them.

"I didn't see the need," he said. He shifted in his seat. Squirmed? "For that matter, I don't see why it should be a problem."

"Problem? I can assure you, it is *not* a problem." She shook her head and crossed her arms over her chest. Did she sound as pathetic and juvenile as she felt?

"You're acting as if it is," Nate replied.

Apparently so.

She dropped her arms. "All right, it's just that I felt very foolish back there."

Her revelation seemed to take him by surprise. "Why?"

"I felt like I was in the middle of a…a…" Holly gestured with her arms as she searched for the right word. "A lover's quarrel."

"Nadine and I are not…serious."

But apparently they were lovers. Or they had been. That ache was back, and so was the small voice in Holly's head that kept telling her to let the matter drop. It was none of her business. Besides, what right did she have to question Nate's personal relationships when there was a man waiting for her back in Morenci that everyone assumed she would agree to marry in the near future?

Since she couldn't ignore the ache, she ignored the voice and pressed on. "Serious or not, Ms. Masterson clearly was not pleased when she found out that I had spent the night in your home. Has she ever spent the night there?"

She studied his profile. A muscle ticked in his jaw,

telling Holly she'd struck a nerve. "I'm not going to answer that. What I will say is this—I can't help how Nadine feels or what she thinks."

"It doesn't bother you?"

"She and I aren't serious," he said again, this time through clenched teeth.

Holly let out an inelegant snort.

Nate swore and then swerved. The truck left the main road and pulled onto a narrow two-track that was mottled with mud puddles from the previous night's downpour.

Holly braced her hands on the dashboard as they rattled over the rutted road.

"Wh-where are we g-going?"

"To see the secluded beach house that you just rented for a two-week stay."

"Do you mean to tell me there is no proper road?" Apparently the word *secluded* should have been written in capital letters.

"Sure there is. This is what's called a shortcut." He winked, though nothing about his demeanor at the moment was particularly friendly or relaxed.

"Nate, please slow down." Her molars smacked together a couple of times after she said it.

"It's just a little off-roading," he defended. "I wanted to give you a bit of the local experience."

Just then, the truck's front right tire hit an especially deep rut. Mud splattered the windshield and the side of the vehicle. Unfortunately for Holly, she hadn't had either the foresight or the time to roll up her window. Great gobs of thick brown matter rained in on her.

She let out a squeal of outrage befitting both a woman and a princess.

Nate took one look at her—she could imagine what he saw given the condition of her blouse—and expelled an oath aimed at himself. He hastily stopped the vehicle and began handing her napkins that he pulled from the glove box.

"God. Oh, God. I'm really sorry. I…I was going too fast."

"Yes," she said drolly. She pulled down the sun visor and studied herself in the mirror attached to the back of it. She was as speckled as a leopard.

"I am sorry, Holly."

"We've established that." She swiped at the side of her face, succeeding only in making several small spots into one large smudge.

"Are you going to say anything?" Nate asked.

"I believe I have been speaking."

"But not talking. To me." He grabbed a napkin and dabbed at her shirt, stopping just short of her breast. "I'm making it worse."

"No. I don't think it can get worse."

He closed his eyes and sighed before leaning his head back against the rest. "This makes two outfits of yours that I've ruined."

He looked and sounded so miserable that she was left with no choice but to take some pity on him. "What is that saying? You're on a roll."

Nate turned his head and opened one eye. "Can you forgive me?"

"They're just clothes, Nate." She patted her gritty

face. "And I was due for a facial. A mud treatment such as this would set me back quite a bit in Paris."

He laughed. The sound held more relief than humor. "I was being an idiot."

"If you're expecting me to disagree with you…" She let the sentence trail off as a challenge, adding in a pair of arched brows for effect.

"I was mad, okay?"

Holly figured that much out for herself, but over what exactly remained unclear. "Why? Because it was none of my business?"

If he'd said yes, she could have lived with that. In fact, she probably would have apologized, too, because he would have been right.

But what he said instead floored her.

"Nadine and I have gone out on and off for years, even…even during high school."

As in, not long after Holly was out of the picture. She pretended to blot at the splotches on the front of her blouse, when in fact she was pressing against that persistent ache in her heart.

"So, you're high-school sweethearts? That's the term for it, right?"

"Yes." He grabbed her hand. "But no. Nadine and I aren't high-school sweethearts. We're just…just two lonely people waiting for the right person to come along." He squeezed Holly's hand. "I don't want you to get the wrong impression of me. I've broken no promises to Nadine, because I've never made her any. And I've always made it clear, or at least tried to, that we… we're not headed anywhere but where we are right now."

Not my business.

Not my business.

Not my business.

Despite the phrase she chanted over and over again in her head, Holly still heard herself ask Nate, "And where might that be?"

He let go of her hand and scrubbed his face. He took his time answering. When he did, she understood perfectly why he'd hesitated.

"In my case at least, it's waiting for someone I can never have."

CHAPTER SEVEN

NATE knew he'd just dropped one hell of a bomb. Holly's shell-shocked expression confirmed as much. He hadn't meant to say it. Part of him wanted to take it back. But it was a fact. One he couldn't deny while sitting across from the only woman who with whom he'd ever felt like he could conquer the world.

Except that he couldn't.

Even assuming she felt the same way, they couldn't have a future together. Morenci's future queen and an American resort owner? Yeah, right. That would never fly.

He glanced over at Holly, who was staring out the window in silence. He wasn't sure what he expected her to say. It certainly wasn't, "I'm seeing someone, too."

Which is what she told him a moment later.

"Ah. Oh. Right." He'd read the news stories, of course. He nodded, not sure what else to say. After all, it made sense. She was halfway through her twenties, the heiress to not just a vast fortune, but to an actual kingdom. She would be expected to marry. He swallowed thickly. And carry on the royal lineage.

On the seat beside him, Holly was saying softly, "He is a nice man. Kind. And very bright."

They were the right words, perfectly acceptable adjectives considering the subject matter, but Nate found the way Holly was studying her hands to be far more revealing.

"You don't love him."

"No." She glanced his way. Even though she smiled, he saw the sadness in her eyes.

"But?" he pressed, knowing the conjunction fit into the equation somewhere.

"My mother thinks Phillip is perfect."

Phillip. The guy would have to be named Phillip. It was a very, well…royal and no-nonsense-sounding name. Nate would bet the title to his resort that the guy never went by plain old Phil.

He was probably going to regret it, but he asked, "So, what does this Phillip do for a living?"

"He's a businessman like you," Holly told him. If only she'd left it at that. But, no, she continued with, "His family owns several oil refineries in my country. Since he's taken over from his father, he's put environmental concerns ahead of corporate profits, which earned him the Royal Medal a couple of years ago. That's how we met."

"Wow. The Royal Medal." Morenci's highest honor. Nate ran his tongue over his teeth. "And a green guy to boot, huh?"

"The environment is important."

"You don't have to tell me," he said. The great outdoors was his meal ticket. "So, um, what happens now?"

"I'm not sure." She shook her head slowly. Her gaze fixed on some point in the distance that he was sure she wasn't seeing, she repeated, "I'm not sure."

Had she not looked so miserable, Nate might have pressed.

Instead, he said, "The island is a great place to think."

Then, without another word, he started the truck. Slowly this time, he drove down the two-track, careful to avoid the worst of the ruts.

It took another twenty minutes before the truck emerged from the dappled green canopy of the woods to a small clearing just up from the lake. There was no sandy beach here, but plenty of reeds and water lilies in the bay's rocky shallows. Before that, the landscape was dotted with wildflowers and the occasional poison ivy plant.

"This is pretty," she remarked. The line between her brows softened as she scanned the scene before her. "It would make a lovely painting."

"A watercolor?" That had been her favorite medium.

She nodded, her gaze riveted on the lake. "The way the colors meld together, teals and blues. It's breathtaking."

It *was* breathtaking. This, Nate knew, was exactly why he'd given up skyscrapers and the madness of city living. As much as he'd thought he'd wanted an urban lifestyle after growing up on a speck of land in the middle of one of the Great Lakes, the truth was he was small-town at heart. He wouldn't make any apologies for that. He glanced over at Holly, noting the rapturous expression on her face, and he knew she wasn't expecting one.

* * *

She started toward the lake.

"Just watch where you walk." Once he had her attention, he pointed out the three-leafed plant that could cause a couple weeks of grief to those who came into contact with it. They both knew that from personal experience.

Once they were almost to the shore, he turned Holly to the right. The chalet was a couple hundred feet down the shore from them. A man and a woman sat on the lower deck. The current occupants were making good use of the gas grill. The scent of sizzling steaks wafted on the breeze along with their laughter.

"That's where you'll be staying."

"Oh, it is lovely."

"And a good hiding place."

His assessment made her frown. "I'm not running away," she insisted.

"Getting away."

She nodded and murmured what sounded like, "Thinking."

"I'm there." He pointed across the bay to where the green tin roof of his lakefront cottage glinted in the sunlight.

Holly turned to him. On a smile, she said, "We'll be next-door neighbors, of a fashion."

"I guess so." He reached out to scratch at a patch of dried mud on her nose.

"I'm a mess."

"A pretty mess," he clarified, resisting the urge to drop a kiss on the very nose he'd just tried to rid of dirt.

"I need to get cleaned up."

Nate nodded. She was right, of course. He should

take her back to his cottage where she could shower while he swung by the marina. He'd been gone several hours. In the meantime, a couple of yachts were due in today, one of them making the Saint Lawrence loop that took the big crafts from the open waters of the Atlantic Ocean all the way inland to the Great Lakes system. This one was out of Fort Myers, Florida, and was destined for Chicago.

Despite his responsibilities back at the marina, Nate said, "Lake's right there."

"Excuse me?"

"The lake." He nodded in its direction a second time. "It's still a bit chilly this time of year." In fact, this far north, it rarely became anything other than what the polite termed *refreshing*. With a grin, he added, "But I never knew you to mind a cool dip."

"Are you daring me, Nathaniel Matthews?"

How was it he found her arched eyebrows and use of his full name so damned sexy?

His first genuine smile in days unfurled. "Yes, ma'am. I believe I am."

Her chin rose. "I don't like to swim alone. In fact, that was my grandmother's rule."

"Swim with a buddy," he finished for her before his throat closed.

"So…" Holly blinked guilelessly at him as she backed toward the water, shedding her shoes as she went. "Will you be my buddy, Nate?"

I'll be anything you damn well want me to be, he nearly replied.

But that would be foolish, not to mention presumptuous. Holly wasn't asking him to be anything but a friend. She had someone waiting for her back in her country. Someone she might not love, but who was far more suitable to her station in life.

He reminded himself of that fact again and again as he watched her wade backward into the water, her smile as tempting as a siren's song. He found it didn't matter. He loved seeing her like this: smiling, having fun and acting very much like the girl she'd once been.

Except she was all woman now.

Awareness pummeled Nate as the waves lapped gently at Holly's body, first wetting her calves and then her thighs. Soon enough, the capri pants she had on were soaked. They stuck to her body like a second skin, tugging a groan from deep in his chest. Need built inside him, even more fierce than the likes of which he'd experienced the evening before when he'd kissed her. Nate decided it was just as well that when the water reached her waist, Holly turned and dove under.

She bobbed to the surface a few feet away. Then she stood. It was all Nate could do to remain on his feet—his knees felt that weak.

The water was just below her breasts now. And the blouse she wore had turned all but translucent, molding to her curves. The water was *very* cold indeed.

He held his breath as she leaned over and used her cupped hand to splash some of it on her face and hair, removing the last traces of mud.

"Aren't you coming in?" she called to him as she straightened.

Any other woman and he would have been galloping through the surf at that invitation. But this was Holly. If Nate waded in to where she stood, he would want to touch her. He would *need* to touch her, he amended silently. Just as he had the other night. And if he touched her...

Well, it wouldn't be a good idea. For either of them. He decided to leave it at that, even though his imagination was, at that very moment, busy filling in all of the blanks.

"Nah. I'll sit this one out. I can be your buddy from here."

He lowered himself onto a stump, watching enviously as she played in the surf.

Lucky water. Lucky waves.

A moment later, she waded ashore, wringing out her hair and the ends of her blouse as she came.

"All better," she announced, gingerly picking her way through the rocks and vegetation.

Nate begged to differ, but he merely nodded.

When she reached him, her brows drew together. "Nate, didn't you warn me to watch out for poison ivy around here?"

"Sure did." He repeated the old saw: "Leaves of three, leave 'em be."

She pressed a finger to her lower lip. "I fear you may be surrounded by it."

He glanced about only a second before launching himself off the log. Damn, if she wasn't right. How could he have missed it, trained outdoorsman as he was? But, of course, he knew. He'd been distracted.

Very, very distracted.

To her credit, Holly didn't tease him for the faux pas he hadn't made in a dozen years. Nor did she laugh. She didn't even crack a smile. Though, from her expression, he could tell it was costing her. Nate did the only thing that he could under the circumstances. He forgot all about dignity and decorum. With a whoop suitable to the Native American warriors who had long ago occupied the island, he made a beeline for the water, stripping off his shirt and shedding his shoes as he ran. He could only hope that any of the plant's oil on his body would be washed away before an allergic reaction had time to get started.

He blasted through the shallows, despite the rocky bottom, and headed for the drop-off he remembered to the far right of where they'd come in. Just at the threshold of where the water changed from aquamarine to deep blue, he tucked himself into a ball, launched himself in the air and hollered, "Geronimo!"

Unfortunately, his launch turned out to be a bit premature. In his defense, it had been a long time since Nate had done a cannonball at this actual site. Years, in fact. He landed on his bottom end with a thud just shy of the deep water. Thank God he was still wearing his shorts or his butt would have endured a sandpapering the likes of which the old cabinets in some of the resort's cabins had endured prior to being refinished.

"I give you a six," Holly hollered from the shore. She was holding up the corresponding number of fingers and grinning madly.

She looked adorable and desirable, two adjectives Nate normally wouldn't put together. But this *was* Holly. Just that quickly, he was sucked back in time. Foolish though he knew it to be, he called, "Come on out, sunshine, and show me what a ten looks like."

She planted her hands on her hips, her smile just this

side of jaunty. "Do you really think you can handle the embarrassment, Matthews?"

Though he could reach the bottom, he flipped onto his back and floated as if he hadn't a care in the world. And, damn, if he didn't feel that way at the moment.

"Bring it on," he challenged.

She dashed through the surf, grinning like a kid the entire time. No one would mistake her for a princess just then, Nate thought. Idly, he wondered what old Phil would think. When she reached the drop-off, she executed a perfect tuck-and-launch before disappearing under the water.

Oh, yeah. A definite ten.

Then she rose up from the water like some damned mermaid, flipping back the honeyed locks of her long hair, and he doubled the score.

"So?" she asked.

He waded toward her and took the plunge. Literally. The lake bottom fell away and Nate found himself treading water, his arms reaching for and then reeling in the one woman who filled his fantasies, but who could never fulfill the dreams he'd almost forgotten existed.

"You're a ten," he said truthfully, as they treaded water together.

"Really? I haven't lost my touch?"

"Not in the least." Then, even though Nate called himself a dozen kinds of fool, he kissed her.

Holly forgot to kick her legs. Come to that, she forgot to breathe. They wound up submerged, mouths locked together. Desire like she'd only allowed herself to imagine washed over her, as insistent as the waves.

Nate kicked upward, taking them to the surface, where they both gasped for air. Even so, they remained locked in an embrace—an embrace suited to lovers, given the way their bodies were pressed tightly together. His warmth helped take away the lake water's chill.

The first word Holly managed was not *thanks* or even *sorry*. Rather, it was "Please."

It was a foolish plea. Please what? She wasn't sure she had an answer for herself, let alone one for Nate. Thus it came as a relief when he didn't ask her for clarification. Instead, he kicked sideways, one arm jutting out in powerful sidestrokes that moved them inland. Before she knew it, her feet were once again planted on the seabed. They rose together. She felt oddly vulnerable, naked in a way that went beyond her soaked clothes. And one glance down had her cringing. Good heavens, her shirt was nearly see-through and the bra she was wearing wasn't much better.

Embarrassment made sense right now. But another emotion lingered with it, oddly reminiscent of the feeling she'd gotten when she'd secretly chartered a jet to America and then asked Henry to drive her to the airport.

On the shore, they picked up their discarded shoes and headed for the truck in silence. All the while awareness taunted her. The man looked good in wet cargo shorts, better, in fact, than most men of her acquaintance managed to look outfitted in designer attire.

Nate pulled a folded blanket from the truck bed,

shaking leaves and debris from it before handing it to Holly.

"You're probably cold." He cleared his throat.

Holly felt her cheeks grow warm. Yes, that much *was* obvious. Gratefully, she pulled it around her body and slipped into the truck's cab. In addition to her breasts' embarrassing reaction to the chilly water, her teeth were chattering and her skin was prickled with gooseflesh, which was why she found it amazing that she still felt on fire.

The drive back to the main road was quiet. Nate drove slowly this time, glancing sideways with each rut they hit. Holly never said a word. She didn't complain. She didn't tease. She simply remained silent, her hands gripping the edges of the blanket around her. He could only imagine what she was thinking. God, he'd screwed up royally. No pun intended.

He hadn't meant to kiss her. Again. He knew better after that kiss the night before. But once she'd been in his arms, her body pressed against his... He swallowed thickly now.

I'm not a saint.

But it was more than his lack of restraint that was the issue here. It was the woman. Holly was his first love, and even though Nate had long tried to deny it, she was his *only* love. Which was why he would both treasure and regret kissing her today. This was a memory that would haunt him long after the woman was gone.

He had barely pulled the truck to a stop outside his cottage and she had already unbuckled her seat belt and was reaching for the door handle.

"If you could telephone Hank while I change my clothes, I would appreciate it," she called over her shoulder as she headed into the house.

The screen door squawked open before slamming closed behind her. Nate sighed heavily. So, she really did plan to return to the mainland for the time between now and when she could check in at the chalet. It made sense. Perfect sense. What didn't make sense was the fact that Nate sat on his deck, sipping a beer, rather than making the requested phone call.

Holly was only in America for a short time, he rationalized as he waited for her. That was long enough to disturb his peace, but not nearly long enough to satisfy his curiosity or his interest. He was being selfish perhaps, and definitely foolish, but he wanted as much of her as he could have, even if afterward her memory made him ache.

Besides, for a little while this afternoon, she'd looked so carefree and happy. Her laughter had echoed across the bay, every bit as enchanting as the loon's call first thing on quiet mornings. He liked knowing that he had a hand in that. Taking another sip of beer, he decided that perhaps his reasons weren't so selfish after all.

Half an hour later, he was still sitting in his favorite lounge chair, staring out at the view, when she opened the sliding glass door and joined him. She'd pulled her hair into a simple ponytail and had changed into a pair of crisp tan walking shorts. The blouse she wore was red, with rolled-up cuffs that buttoned just above her elbows.

"So, what time did Hank say he would be here?" she inquired.

Nate glanced past her. Just inside the house was the same stack of luggage with which she'd arrived the day before.

Had it really been a mere day since Nate's life had been turned upside down? In less than twenty-four hours he'd gone from wishing she'd never come to wishing she never had to leave. He'd never been much of a fan of roller coasters, but he'd ride this one to the end.

"He, uh, can't." Nate rose upon saying so. It felt wrong to remain seated when offering a lie.

Holly blinked. "He can't."

"Sorry. No. His plane is booked. For the next few days, in fact." Nate marveled at his talent for lying. If only he were this good when it came to playing poker with the guys. He would have been able to pay cash for the parcel of land just up the beach, rather than having had to jump through hoops to secure a bank loan.

"Another pilot, perhaps?"

"Hank said the pilots he would recommend are busy right now." He hunched his shoulders. "Apparently, the storm threw schedules off."

Holly's expression darkened as reality set in. "Oh. Oh, my."

"It's all right. You can stay here until Sunday." Nate felt the need to restrain his hands by putting them into the pockets of his still damp shorts when he added, "As my guest. In the, um, guest room."

Also known as his boyhood bedroom. Fantasy central.

"I don't know."

She nibbled her lower lip. God help him, Nate wanted

to do the same. Instead, he reminded her, "You slept in there last night."

"Yes, but…" She gestured with her hand. "Hank."

Ah, yes. Their snoring chaperone.

Guilt nipped at him only a little when he said, "Holly, come on. Despite what just went on at the lake, you can trust me."

She looked abashed. "Of course I can. I didn't mean to imply otherwise. It's just…"

"Just what?"

They eyed one another for a moment. Then she leveled him with her words.

"I don't know that I can trust myself."

Nate did the only thing a man could do after a beautiful woman offered up a declaration like that. He hightailed it to his pickup truck and sped away. In this case, only a short distance away. Specifically, to the resort's marina, even though it was close enough to walk.

Good God! What was he getting himself into? After slowly making its way to the top, that roller coaster he was riding was not only taking a steep plunge, but also threatening to go off the tracks.

Holly didn't trust herself around Nate?

He'd be lying if he claimed that wasn't music to his ears. His ego wasn't hurting at the moment, either, though other parts of him were damned uncomfortable, and not all of them could be found in his shorts. But he'd gone through this once before with her. He'd gotten involved, put his heart on the line. It had wound up good and busted.

The difference this time, Nate reminded himself,

was that he would be going in with his eyes wide open, well aware that the odds were stacked against anything long-term. Sure, Holly was eager for a simpler life and confused about her supposed engagement to a man her mother had all but handpicked for her. But none of that meant she and Nate had a future together.

How would that work anyway? Which one of them would move? She couldn't very well govern her country while living in his. And he couldn't imagine giving up his blissfully low-key lifestyle to live in Morenci's stylish capital city and run with the jet set.

The twins were at the marina when he entered the shop, which also served as the resort's front desk. So was Mick Langley, who'd worked the main cash register since Nate was a toddler.

The man's hair was solid gray now and his big hands gnarled with arthritis. He was past the age of retirement. Well past it. But he put in a full day's work five days a week and he never complained. Heck, even on his days off he could be found somewhere on the resort grounds. He loved the place as much as Nate did.

"Hey, Nate."

"Mick." He glanced out at the marina, where a couple of big cabin cruisers were moored in the outermost slips. "Those yachts get in without incident?"

"Yep. The Burns brothers might be young, but they've been taught well."

"Thanks to you."

The older man acknowledged the compliment with a shrug. "They're an asset to the resort. So are you. You've done your folks proud."

"Thanks."

Nate wondered what his parents would think if they knew Holly was back. They'd liked her. They'd also witnessed his heartache.

"They comin' for a visit anytime soon?" Mick asked.

"I spoke to my mom a couple days ago. They're thinking the end of July, but no firm plans have been made yet. Dad's playing in a local golf tournament."

It seemed his dad was always playing in a golf tournament these days, Nate thought fondly.

"Be good to seem 'em." Mick nodded.

"Yes."

Eager for something to occupy his mind, Nate went behind the counter and scanned the day's receipts. They'd rented out two fishing boats and a handful of canoes thanks to the calm waters after the storm. Bicycle rentals were up, too.

He tucked the receipts back in the drawer. "Anything else I need to know about?"

"Not really." Mick scratched one wiry sideburn then and snorted. "Gave out a lot of free bait today."

Nate nodded. "I figured our guests deserved a little perk after the storm knocked out the cable."

"I'd say that was a good call. Been a lot of fishing from the dock today. Adults, kids… In my book that sure beats sitting around watching the boob tube anyday."

Holly had liked fishing. She'd even baited her own hook back in the day.

"They catch anything?" Nate asked.

"Sure did. Saw a few of them haul in some serious keepers."

"Yeah?" Half his mouth crooked up in a smile, even as his mind wandered again to the "keeper" he'd pulled out of the bay a few hours earlier.

"A couple twelve-inch perch," the older man said.

"Hmm. Not bad."

"And a sixteen-inch rock bass."

Nate blinked at that. "Off the marina dock. Really?"

Mick was nodding. "A kid of about ten hauled that one up, and with a bamboo pole of all things. No proper reel even. Even the old-timers who camp out at the end of the dock were impressed."

"And a little envious, I bet."

"Yep. That kind of luck and the good memories of today will bring the family back next year."

Which gave Nate an idea.

The older man's expression soured, but Nate was only half listening as Mick launched into a lengthy complaint about the cormorants he'd seen earlier on a sandbar a hundred yards off the marina. The diving birds could ruin a good fishing spot.

Nate was busy putting together some supplies. The rod he selected offered good flex. The reel wasn't top-of-the-line, but it would do the job. He had bobbers, sinkers and hooks in the tackle box back at his house. As well as the other equipment necessary to do a little recreational fishing.

Meanwhile, Mick had wound himself up good. "Damned birds are pests!" Next he would be declaring that they should be shot on sight regardless of their protection under the federal law as migratory fowl.

Nate glanced over at him when Mick became silent. A frown wrinkled the older man's forehead.

"What are you doing there? Something happen to that fancy rod and reel of yours?"

"This is for someone else. A guest." Nostalgia had him smiling. "She used to be one hell of an angler."

"She forget to bring her stuff this trip?"

"Something like that," Nate replied.

Mick seemed to accept the explanation. Then he remarked. "I saw you out driving with a girl today. The Burns boys told me she was an old friend of the family."

Nate cleared his throat. "Old friend. Exactly."

Mick looked about as convinced as Nate felt in offering the description. He tried again. "Holly. You remember her." How could anyone forget her? "She, um, used to come here with her grandmother when she was a kid."

Mick's eyes narrowed. "That skinny little kid with the funny accent?"

Nate nearly choked on his laughter. He figured Holly would be as amused by the description as he was. "That's one way to describe her. She wasn't from around these parts." He coughed and added a vague "Europe."

"Europe?"

Let's not go there. So, Nate redirected. "Yes, but her grandmother was from Texas. Add those two locations together and it's no wonder you thought she talked a little funny."

The older man was nodding, "Sure, sure. I remember her now. The grandmother was a looker. I seem to remember some talk…" Mick's words trailed off and he glanced sharply at Nate.

"The island gets under people's skin. Once they've come here, experienced it, they always find their way back."

"I'd say so." Mick's expression was knowing.

CHAPTER EIGHT

SHE was the one seated on the deck enjoying a beer when he arrived home a couple of hours later. Any awkwardness she might have felt evaporated when she spied the fishing pole.

Her eyes lit up like a kid's at Christmas. "Is that for me?"

Nate nodded. "I didn't figure you had remembered to pack your fishing pole."

He'd attached the reel at the marina. It just needed tackle and some bait and she would be ready to cast the line into the bay.

"It's perfect."

"It's a fishing pole."

"Yes, but you're the only person I know who would think to give me one."

From her tone and glowing expression he knew she meant that as a compliment.

"Thank you."

"You're welcome."

"Can we go fishing?"

"Right now?"

Some of her excitement dimmed. "I'm sorry. You probably have other things to do."

He couldn't think of one. For that matter, even if he did, he would have cleared his schedule, just to see her eyes light up again.

"It's not that, Holly. It's the license. We used to sell them at the marina, but since the state Department of Natural Resources and Environment started leasing office space from us last summer, we decided to leave that to them."

"They're closed for the day," she ventured.

"Besides, the best fishing around here is in the morning off the marina dock."

"I guess I can wait." She leaned the pole against the cedar siding. "Patience is a virtue, or so I've been told."

Patience. Nate was feeling anything but at the moment. Need growled along with his stomach.

"Dinner," he blurted out. "We should eat."

Holly claimed not to be hungry, but she was a guest in his home, under his care, and he knew she hadn't eaten much all day. Now it was past seven o'clock.

Briefly, Nate considered making spaghetti. He was quite capable of boiling water, cooking pasta and heating up sauce from a jar. Chop up some lettuce for a salad, add in some garlic toast and it was a tasty and filling meal. One that had been a staple of his diet during college. It still was when he chose to eat in. But spaghetti—even paired with a salad and some garlic bread, neither of which he had on hand—wouldn't address the main issue.

If they stayed in, they would be alone. No chaperones. No excuses to heed. As much as Nate wanted to be with Holly, he didn't want to rush things. That roller coaster be damned. She wasn't the only one who didn't trust herself.

"How about we go out?" he asked.

"If that's what you want."

What he wanted? Nate bit back a groan. He wasn't going to go there.

"Out. Definitely." He hitched a thumb over his shoulder. "I'm just going to change my, uh…" He motioned to his clothing, wondering what he had in his closet besides T-shirts that didn't require an iron's attention.

Her brow crinkled. "Should I change as well?"

"No." She was perfect just as she was.

Upstairs, Nate decided on a quick shower and, after a glance at his reflection in the mirror, a shave. He took a little extra care with his hair, adding in some styling gel that the woman who regularly cut his hair had recommended. He was overdue for a cut, so he hoped it would tame the worst of his waves. While he was at it, he gargled with a mint-flavored mouthwash and slapped on some cologne whose cap was layered in dust from disuse.

In his bedroom closet, he found a pair of khaki shorts. No cargo pockets on the sides of these. He added a pale blue button-down shirt. He could have left it untucked, but he decided to go the more formal route, which required him to add a belt. Sandals and sneakers were out. Nate had a pair of deck shoes…somewhere. He found them under his bed surrounded by dust bunnies.

"You look very nice," Holly said when he came downstairs. "And do I smell cologne?"

Nate felt heat gather in his cheeks. "I showered," he said by way of explanation.

"Your hair looks different, too."

He shrugged. "Combed it."

"Very debonair." She tucked away a smile. She was teasing him.

"I may not be Prince Charming, but I don't always look like a beach bum."

It sounded like she said, "Who wants Prince Charming?" But she'd turned away to collect her purse from the couch.

In the truck she asked, "Are we going to the Fishing Hole? I wasn't old enough to get in there the last time I was on the island."

Nate shook his head. "I was thinking of something a little less rowdy. There's a place called Beside the Bay that has a great outside patio."

It catered to the yacht crowd and high-end tourists who rented out high-end homes, such as the one Holly would be staying in. It was by far the fanciest establishment on the island, with a Cordon Bleu-trained chef and a stellar wine selection.

"Is the restaurant new?"

"Pretty new." He nodded. "But it's been in business for half a dozen years."

Beside the Bay was done in what designers would call rustic chic. The building itself was Frank Lloyd Wright-inspired with an iron roof. Hanging baskets and pots that were overflowing with flowers welcomed diners to its entry at the end of a flagstone path that led from the parking lot.

They were shown to a table at the interior of the restaurant, away from the big windows that looked out onto the lake. That was a bit of a disappointment, since the view was five-star.

Even as Holly was resigning herself to a seat indoors, Nate was asking their hostess, whom he of course knew, "Would it be a problem, Danielle, if my friend and I were to dine outside this evening?"

"Not at all, Nate."

Only a couple of other tables were occupied on the deck, and the people sitting at those were sipping drinks rather than dining. But a smiling waiter brought them a couple of menus a few minutes later and took their drink order. Nate requested an imported beer. Holly went with white wine.

"This is a lovely spot for dinner, Nate. Thank you."

"The view is hard to compete with, but the food is pretty good, too." Curiosity had him asking, "What kind of places do you frequent back home? Are you still a fan of pepperoni pizza?"

"I am." She laughed. "Not that there are many places in Morenci that serve the kind found here in the States." Holly leaned closer and in a low voice confided, "For my sixteenth birthday, my grandmother had a pizzeria send me a dozen pies via airmail."

"I'm thinking they probably weren't still hot when they arrived."

"They were frozen. I ate one a week for three months, despite my mother's warnings that the grease would make my face break out."

"So, if you don't hang out at the local pizzeria, where do you go to eat?"

"I don't dine out very often," she admitted. "Not at

restaurants at least. Mostly, when I'm not eating in, I'm at some sort of official function, a charity ball or state dinner. The food is wonderful, of course, but…it's not the same."

"That's because it's work."

She glanced up. "Yes. Exactly."

"That must be hard."

"It's…expected."

"Doesn't make it less difficult."

"No."

The waiter arrived with their drinks and took their entrée orders. They'd decided to forgo an appetizer since their meals came with salads and a cup of the day's soup. They both went with blackened lake trout.

Once they were alone again, Nate asked, "So, where do you and Phillip go on an evening out?"

"Actually, Phillip and I rarely appear in public unless it's at official events."

Hence the swirl of rumors regarding the serious nature of their relationship, he guessed.

"So, you dine in?"

"Yes. At the palace. And…"

"His home?" he finished for her.

Holly nodded, her gaze riveted to the lake. The sun was just starting to lower over the bay, but he doubted that was what captivated her attention. "In addition to his family's estates in Morenci, he has a lovely villa in the south of France."

Despite her rather unimpressed tone, Nate's head felt as if it would explode. He wasn't going to try to compete with the guy. There was no reason to, but still…

A small voice reminded him that Holly didn't love

Phillip. As much as Nate wanted to latch onto that, he couldn't help wondering if she could be happy living a different lifestyle. One slower-paced and far more casual. And not just for a couple of weeks, but 24/7? Even as he was telling himself that some things just weren't meant to be, he was recalling her expression when he'd given her the fishing pole.

Before either of them could speak again, a woman appeared at their table. She was older, a little on the plump side, and carried in her hands a little dog that was outfitted with more bling than most Hollywood starlets wore on Oscar night.

There was a good bit of the South in her drawl when she said, "I hate to interrupt your dinner, young lady, but I just have to say what a striking resemblance you bear to Princess Hollyn of Morenci."

"That's very kind of you," Holly replied, neither acknowledging her true identity nor denying it.

"Oh, my gosh! And you talk like her, too!" the woman exclaimed with such excitement it caused her little dog to start yipping.

The other diners glanced their way. Nate's stomach pitched and rolled. This was it. She was exposed. Holly, on the other hand, appeared unaffected.

In a confidential tone, she said, "I'll let you in on a little secret."

"Yes?" The older woman leaned in eagerly.

"I'm a celebrity impersonator."

The woman's eyes widened. "You're kidding."

"No. I make a good living at it, too. I think it's my accent that clinches it for me. I've worked for years to perfect it."

"It's very good. You had me fooled."

"Not to brag, but my agent tells me I'm the best of the bunch."

"Oh, you are," the other woman gushed. "You absolutely are."

"Thank you for saying so. It's always good to hear from an objective person. My mother, of course, thinks I'm spot on." Holly shrugged. "But she's my mother. What else is she supposed to think?"

The woman nodded before casting a sheepish glance Nate's way. "I'm sorry to have interrupted your dinner." Her gaze back on Holly, she said, "I was going to ask for your autograph and to see if you wanted to take a picture with me."

"Really? I'm so flattered."

"But since you're not who I thought you were…" The woman's cheeks flamed scarlet. "I mean, I'd be happy to have my picture taken with you anyway."

"That's kind, but I think you should aim your camera lens at that incredible view." Holly pointed to the lake, where the sun was starting to set. "It's far more memorable than I am, believe me."

"I think I'll do just that," the woman agreed. "Thank you, by the way."

"For?"

"Being so gracious. I've approached real celebrities who weren't half as kind and patient as you are, and you're not anyone." She coughed delicately. "Well, you know what I mean."

"I do. And the pleasure was mine."

Holly was grinning from ear to ear when the woman left.

"I'd say you handled that encounter like a pro," Nate told her.

"I was feeling inspired." Holly shrugged then. "Besides, if I had been rude or standoffish, it only would have raised her suspicions."

"Is that the only reason you weren't rude or standoffish?" he asked.

"Of course not. People are curious. Most of them, such as that woman, mean no harm. They are what you would call starstruck."

Nate grinned. "You make a good celebrity impersonator, by the way. Do you do that often?"

"Actually, that was a first for me."

"Really?"

"I'm not often without a royal escort. Still, it seemed like a good idea in this instance," Holly explained. "After all, she had me pegged. Flat-out denial only would have made it worse. This way, she feels like she's part of the deception."

It was hard not to marvel at Holly's cleverness and composure. "She didn't even want to snap your photograph."

"Exactly."

He liked her all the more for the jaunty smile she beamed at him afterward. There was so much of that young girl he remembered still inside her.

Their drinks arrived along with a basket of freshly baked rolls and their salads.

Nate raised his beverage in a toast. "To a rising star."

Holly clinked her wineglass against his beer glass, but she set it back on the table without taking a sip. She seemed circumspect when she said, "I am hardly a star.

I was born into my position and the corresponding celebrity. I've done nothing to earn either."

"I don't know about that. I mean, the position part, I'll give you. You were born into the role of princess. Call it fate or luck or whatever. But how you choose to act in public and use celebrity is entirely up to you."

"It's a lot of responsibility." He saw her swallow and her shoulders sagged a little, as if bowing under the weight of that responsibility.

"It's a lot of power, too," he said quietly.

"I have no power, Nate. I can't even decide my own future." Her laughter was surprisingly sardonic. She must have realized it. She added in a tone more suited to a civics teacher, "The royal family's role in Morenci is purely ceremonial and has been for more than a century. We don't set policy or make laws."

"But you still wield a lot of influence, Holly. It's up to you how you choose to use it. I think you know that, which is why you've been a voice for orphans in some of the world's poorest countries and championed access to education for girls in cultures that traditionally reserve that right only for boys."

"You've been reading up on me, I see." She leveled the accusation playfully, but a hint of embarrassment stained her cheeks as she reached for one of the warm rolls.

"I've followed your life over the years," he admitted. Odd, but a day ago no one would have been able to force Nate to make such a confession. Now, he continued, "I wondered how you were and what your life was like when the public wasn't watching. I wondered, you know, if you were okay."

In the images of her that he'd seen on television or in print she'd seemed so reserved, so...lifeless.

"You were worried about me?" She broke off a piece of roll.

Dangerous territory, he decided, but he answered truthfully. "I was." As mad as he'd been, and as hurt, he'd also been concerned.

"I wondered if you were all right as well. And if... if you'd forgiven me."

He hadn't. Until she'd returned. Holding a grudge made even less sense than holding on to the tender feelings he had for her. But those tender feelings, he knew, would be much harder to set free.

"I'm not mad anymore. You did what you felt you had to do, maybe even what was for the best. But I wish you'd sent that letter you told me you'd written. I wish I would have heard it from you rather than seeing you in a televised special on European royalty not long after you'd turned sixteen."

She pinched her eyes closed. "I am sorry."

"It's the past, Holly." He reached across the table, found her hand and gave it a squeeze. "What do you say we just concentrate on the here and now."

"The here and now," she repeated. She reached for her wine, and this time after their glasses clinked together, she took a sip.

With both the past and the future put out of mind, they enjoyed the rest of their meal. The conversation centered mainly on small talk, but it veered into personal territory enough that it was impossible not to enjoy himself. She was fun and funny, smart and interesting. She was, in short, every bit as remarkable as he remembered her being.

Once they left the restaurant, his hand slipped to the small of her back. Nate had to remind himself this wasn't a date. Indeed, the very reason he'd taken Holly out was to avoid being alone with her. Of course, now, night had fallen and they were heading back to his quiet cottage. Together.

The easy conversation they'd enjoyed during dinner was long gone by the time he pulled the truck to a stop and came around to open Holly's door.

"Thank you again for dinner," she said once they were inside the cottage.

They both glanced uncertainly toward the stairs. "You're welcome."

"Maybe tomorrow you'll let me treat you."

She'd offered tonight. He'd refused. It wasn't pride, or even the fact that she was female that had caused him to do so. Rather, the old-fashioned belief drilled into him by his mother that when one had a guest under one's roof, one picked up the tab.

Just as his mother had drummed it into Nate's head that a man never pressed or pressured a woman.

"Maybe," he replied, to stave off an argument.

She nodded. "I…I'm rather tired. I think I'll turn in."

"It's been a long day," he agreed.

"Especially for you. I only woke up around noon." It was half past nine now. "You were up much earlier, I would imagine."

"That I was."

"Nate…" She took a step toward him.

He resisted doing the same. That foot and half of

space between them was the only thing keeping his hormones in check. "Good night, Holly."

Holly nodded in understanding. "Good night."

She wasn't halfway up the stairs before Nate knew he would be sleeping outside on the deck.

It was the only place he trusted himself to be with Holly under his roof.

And didn't it just figure, as miserable as he already felt, the first itchy welts from the poison ivy had started to appear on his calves.

Holly didn't know how she managed it, but she spent the following night within easy reach of Nate Matthews without, well, ever *reaching* for him.

To think her mother felt Holly needed to work on her self-control. Olivia would be amazed—and, no doubt, relieved.

Of course, it helped immensely that after that first night when she and Nate dined together, they barely saw one another. Friday morning, she awoke to find him gone, and a blanket and pillow taking up space on one of the deck's lounge chairs. He'd slept there, she knew. Because she'd heard his footsteps on the stairs not only coming up, but also going down a moment later as she'd lain awake holding her breath and foolishly wishing he would tap at her door.

That evening, he came home well after dark, although he thoughtfully had one of the island's delis deliver a meal for her to eat. She dined alone on the deck, trying to take delight in the view, but missing his company.

The public thought she had it made. She felt no bitterness over that fact. Now. Interestingly, nor did she feel the old sense of resignation.

She'd come to Heart Island for a last reprieve. Literally, for a final bit of time in the sun before taking on the latest yoke of royal responsibility: marriage and the whole business of begetting heirs.

Holly had thought that coming here would make it easier to accept her future. But if anything, seeing Nate again and stealing romantic moments that both of them likely would live to regret had only made it more difficult.

Given the way he was avoiding her, she figured he felt the same way.

It didn't help when Nadine arrived at the cottage on Saturday, Holly's final night. The other woman came, ostensibly, to deliver the keys to the place Holly had rented on the other side of the bay, even though Holly wouldn't be able to check in until the following afternoon. But the way she glanced around spoke volumes. She perceived Holly as a threat.

If only.

"Nate isn't here," Holly said. She folded her hands at her waist and smiled her most serene smile. Oh, what it cost her on the inside.

"Oh, I wasn't expecting to find him home. I saw his truck up at the marina."

"Then what were you hoping to find?" Holly's face began to ache beneath the smile.

"I don't know what you mean." The other woman blinked innocently.

Holly blinked back. "Oh. I'm sorry. I must have been mistaken."

Nadine expelled a breath then. "No. I'm the one who's sorry. I...I've been curious."

"About?" Holly asked, even though she was sure she knew.

"You and Nate and..." She swept her hand in an arc. "And your living arrangements."

"Sleeping arrangements, I believe, is what you really mean."

Nadine had the grace to grimace and then to apologize again. "I'm sorry. You seem like a very nice person and you've already told me that you and Nate have known each other since childhood. I must seem a little pathetic."

"Not at all." *Suspicious and territorial, certainly. But not pathetic.* Holly would feel the same way if she were in the other woman's shoes.

"Nate might have mentioned that we date."

"He did. Yes."

"It's not serious."

He'd told her that, too. "But you would like it to be," Holly said sympathetically.

"Yes." Nadine fiddled with the band of her wristwatch. "We get along very well, Nate and I. We like a lot of the same things—movies, food, you name it. But I've always sensed that he was holding back."

She glanced up at Holly then. Nadine no longer looked like the successful businesswoman she was, or the jealous, sometimes girlfriend who'd brashly come calling on a potential threat. Now, she just looked vulnerable...and uncertain.

She was saying, "I told myself it was just a typical case of commitment phobia and that eventually he would come around. But…"

Holly waited silently for the other woman to continue. What could she say? *Don't worry about me as competition. Even if Nate does have feelings for me, they can never come to anything.*

"I think he loves you," Nadine announced. "I think he's always loved you."

Holly's mouth dropped open, but the denial drumming in her head never made it to her lips. And, even though she knew it was foolish and hopeless, her heart thunked almost painfully in her chest.

He loves me.

The door opened then. At the threshold stood the man in question, his expression wary as he divided his gaze between the pair of them.

"Hi."

"Nate!" Nadine pasted a smile on her face that did nothing to camouflage her guilt. "Hi."

He nodded to Holly before saying, "I thought that was your car I saw drive past the marina."

"I…I came to give Holly the key to the place she rented for the next couple weeks."

It was completely plausible. Nate seemed to relax. For her part, Holly held up said key and smiled.

"It will be ready anytime after noon tomorrow. The current occupants have checked out early, but housekeeping hasn't finished up inside yet."

"I'm not in any hurry," Holly said. She flushed immediately. It wasn't exactly the right thing to say.

Nate pointed toward the kitchen. "I just came home

to grab a bite to eat. You're welcome to join me. Both of us."

Holly didn't bother to add that she'd already helped herself to some leftovers from the previous night's take-out.

"Thanks for the offer, but I can't stay. I...have a little work to finish up at the office before I can finally knock off for what remains of the weekend," Nadine explained.

"Okay. Well, good seeing you."

"Yes. You, too. And thanks again for bringing me some business." Nadine worked up what passed for a smile.

"No problem."

Holly turned to him the moment the other woman was out the door. "Are you oblivious or just insensitive?"

"What do you mean?" Nate toed off his shoes slowly, like a man who clearly knew that he'd stepped in something messy.

"Nadine is half in love with you!" Actually wholly in love with him, but Holly sought to leave the poor woman some dignity. After all, she knew how Nadine felt.

His brow furrowed. "Why are you so worked up?"

She didn't have an actual answer for him, at least not one that made sense, so she crossed her arms and remained stoic.

Nate continued. "The other day you were upset over that fact for a different reason, if I'm not mistaken."

He had her there. Holly tried again. "You need to be honest with her."

In an instant, Nate went from being cautiously baffled to angry. "I've been nothing but honest! With her. With you." He jabbed a finger in Holly's direction. "The one I've lied to all along has been myself! I've pretended that I'm over you. Well, guess what, Princess. That's never happened."

His outburst left Holly speechless for a moment. As he raked the hair back from his forehead, she found her voice.

"I just want you to be happy, Nate."

"So, what? You want me to marry Nadine?"

No! Her response was as visceral as his earlier one had been. But what Holly managed to say, and in a tone that was amazingly neutral under the circumstances, was, "If that's what it takes, then yes."

"So, because you're willing to make a lifetime commitment to someone you don't love, I should, too?"

She stepped back as if he'd struck her. Before she could respond, he was already apologizing.

"God, Holly. I'm sorry. That was uncalled for. Our situations are vastly different."

"Yes."

But as Holly laid awake long into the night, she found herself wondering if they had to be.

CHAPTER NINE

NATE was still asleep on the deck when Holly crept downstairs early the next morning and took the cordless telephone from its cradle in the kitchen. She'd reached some conclusions during the long, sleepless night. The first was that she needed to call Phillip.

After speaking to her mother that first night on the island, she'd left a brief comment on his office voice mail, well aware he wouldn't be at work to receive it. It was the act of a coward, she could readily admit. Well, an actual conversation couldn't be put off any longer. In fact, it was something that should have occurred a long time ago, not long after she and Phillip were first introduced. Certainly after he'd first broached the subject of marriage.

Nate was right. Holly wasn't without power. And, while her options might be limited, she wasn't without choices, either. She would not marry a man she didn't love, regardless of how "perfect" her mother and others in Morenci deemed him to be.

Phillip answered in French on the third ring. He'd been raised speaking French, which, along with Italian and English, were all spoken in Morenci. She answered in kind.

"Bonjour."

"Hollyn! God in heaven!" he declared. "I have been so eager for your call."

"Did you not receive my earlier message?" she asked.

"Yes. But it was so brief and you sounded, well, you sounded very unlike yourself. It only served to make me more concerned."

Holly wanted to be touched by his words. She wanted to feel even a glimmer of the warmth that she'd felt upon hearing Nate's confession that he'd been worried about her when she hadn't returned to Heart Island that first summer.

But that great void inside of her remained empty, just as she'd known it would. There was no love to fill it up. Respect and affection were insubstantial as substitutes.

"I must apologize for leaving so abruptly. I've been in touch with my mother and so I am well aware of what an inconvenience my absence has been for everyone."

"Yes, it has been a bit of a trial," he concurred. "But we've managed. The press, they are none the wiser, and I have enjoyed this bit of sport in tricking them."

"Wonderful." What else could she say?

"You will be home soon, yes?"

"Yes."

Too soon for her liking, Holly thought, her gaze on the horizon, where the first fingers of light had stretched over the bay. The scene was so peaceful, she closed her eyes and tried to capture it in her memory.

"Excellent. Excellent. I have an important dinner with some foreign investors on Wednesday. I was hoping that you would accompany me. They asked specifically if you would be there. You know how fascinated some people are with royalty."

Indeed, she did.

"Wednesday?" That was three days away. "I hadn't planned to return by then."

"But you will have been gone nearly a week, Hollyn." His voice took on an impatient edge. "Should your absence continue, well, it will become much more difficult to explain...to everyone. More engagements will have to be postponed or canceled. Your mother assured me—"

Holly was done letting her mother to speak for her, as well-intentioned as Olivia might be. "I am allowed a life of my own," she replied, amazed she'd said so, but in no hurry to take it back.

Her words as well as her tone must have surprised Phillip, too. "Is everything all right?"

"Never better. I am just making it clear that, royal or not, I am allowed to have a life."

"Of course."

But his tone was filled with more bafflement than agreement.

Holly pressed ahead. "I understand that I have obligations, but if I were ill or otherwise indisposed, well, other arrangements would be made."

"Are you ill, *ma chérie*?"

She held back a sigh. "Not how you mean."

"Ah. I think I understand," Phillip replied.

"You do?"

"You are a princess, yes. But a woman first. I have moved slowly with our romance out of deference for your royal position, but perhaps that is not what you've wanted. Perhaps I have been remiss in declaring myself." His tone lowered to an intimate level and he added, "In declaring my feelings."

Alarm bells were going off in Holly's head. Dear God! Surely he didn't think she *wanted* him to declare them? Maybe at one time she'd hoped that hearing pretty words might soften her heart toward him, but they would only further complicate matters now.

She rushed to assure him, "Your feelings have been very clear, Phillip. Indeed, they have been clear from the beginning. I fear, however, I have not been clear in my feelings. I am quite fond of you, certainly. And I have been flattered, very flattered, by your interest and attention these past several months."

"Flattery is not what I was hoping to achieve," he remarked dryly.

"I wish I could tell you that I have...romantic feelings where you are concerned, but I think it is best for me to be honest. I enjoy your company and treasure your friendship, but—"

"Let us leave it at that, *ma chérie*. That way I will have my pride."

"I'm sorry, Phillip. Truly."

"As am I."

Nate shifted on the lounge chair and stifled a moan. His back was killing him. But he didn't care. The conversation he'd just overheard trumped physical discomfort.

He'd averaged a B in French during the four years he'd taken it in high school, and he'd never become fluent. But from Holly's subdued tone and some of the key words he'd picked up on her side of the conversation, it was clear the news she'd delivered to Phillip was not good.

Nate resisted the urge to pump his fist in the air. Such a reaction would have been juvenile. But he didn't try to subdue his grin. As the sun broke over the water, even the wicked itching on his legs from the poison ivy couldn't dampen his good mood.

Holly's bags were once again downstairs and lined up at the side door when he popped in just before noon. While he'd been at the marina office helping Mick with the week's checkouts, both cabins and boat slips, she'd been busy. And not only was her luggage ready, but she'd also brought down her bedding. Now, she sat in his kitchen munching on toast that was closer to black than brown, and drinking a cup of the coffee he'd made before heading out.

"All ready to go, I see. And you even stripped the bed."

"It's what a good guest should do." But then she looked dubious. "Right?"

"Sure." Though Hank had shown no such compunction.

"Nadine called a bit ago and said housekeeping had finished up. I can check in whenever I want."

"Well, then, let's not waste time. It's going to be another gorgeous day. You're going to want to spend it on that fancy deck."

She smiled uncertainly. "Nate."

"Yes?" He wondered if she would bring up her earlier phone conversation. Just as Nate wondered if her breaking things off with Phillip had anything at all to do with him. Regardless, he was glad she was taking a stand and taking back some of the power she'd claimed not to have.

"I…I… If you wouldn't mind stopping at the grocery store in town I would be most grateful. The cottage is stocked with all of the basics such as spices and condiments, from what I've been told, but that I will need to bring my own meals."

He glanced at the burned toast, but resisted asking what she knew of making meals.

"What's that on your legs?" she asked as he toted her bags outside.

"Calamine lotion," he muttered.

"Cala—" She wasn't quite successful at swallowing her laughter.

"Go ahead," he offered. "Get it out of your system."

"I don't know what you mean," she replied innocently, even as amusement shimmered in her eyes.

"You're dying to tease me about catching poison ivy."

"I wouldn't dream of it." He gave her extra points for her serious expression. "Tell me, does it itch as horribly as I remember from my third summer here?"

"Worse," he grumbled, but mostly for effect. The fact was it was hard to remain irritable recalling how absolutely adorable Holly had looked that year dotted with the same pink lotion that now covered the better part of his calves.

Nate accompanied Holly inside the island's small market, leaving her to her shopping while he picked up a few staples of his own. Like most weeks, he'd probably dine out as much as he would dine in, so he didn't bother with much more than the basics: bread, more coffee, a bag of donuts, lunch meat and potato chips and two boxes of cereal. He'd stop to pick up milk on the way back.

"I see you've covered the basic food groups," Holly remarked when they ran into one another in one of the aisles. Where he'd grabbed a handcart, she was pushing one and had it filled with an assortment of fresh fruits and vegetables, homemade bread, cheese, wine and some tasty-looking cuts of meat.

"Do you know how to cook those?" he asked, nodding toward the T-bone steaks.

"I'm not helpless." She sighed and rolled her eyes. But her expression clouded a bit. Perhaps she was recalling burnt toast and bitter coffee.

"I'm just asking."

"And I've answered."

"Two steaks, I see. Are you planning for company?"

"Two steaks. Two meals."

"Ah." He rubbed an ankle against the opposite calf. Damned poison ivy.

"I'm ready to check out if you are."

"After you."

Nate intercepted a few curious glances from other customers as they headed to the checkout. The woman at the cash register was more obvious in her interest, but then Melinda Townsend was the island's biggest gossip. As she ran Holly's purchases over the scanner, she baldly asked, "Are you famous?"

Holly made a tsking noise. When she spoke, she somehow managed to flatten her vowels. Nate thought he even detected a bit of Texas twang when she said, "You know, I get that all the time. People are always thinking I look like some Hollywood starlet or reality TV star."

"You look like that girl from the tabloids." The woman pointed to the magazine rack next to the check-out counter. A picture of Holly taken at an event a few weeks earlier stared back at them. Unless Nate missed his guess that was Phillip in the background.

"She and I have a similar bone structure," Holly agreed. "Don't feel bad. You're not the first person to mistake me for her."

Melinda eyed her. Nate held his breath. Then the woman said, "You're way prettier."

"Well, thank you."

As compliments went, it was an interesting one. Holly had just been told she was more attractive than, well, herself.

"I bet you wish you had her bank account, though," Melinda said. "She's loaded."

"Money can't buy happiness, as the saying goes," Holly replied on a shrug.

"Maybe not, but I wouldn't mind trying to find out." The other woman's laugher boomed. She glanced past Holly to Nate. "What about you, Nate? Would you mind being as rich as a princess?"

He set his handcart down on the conveyor belt behind the last of Holly's purchases. He'd be happy with the princess, rich or not. But what he said was, "I'm content with what I have. It's more than enough."

"That's only because you're not greedy," Melinda said. She sent a wink in Holly's direction. "Nate's a local and his tastes are simple. He's beer and pretzels rather than champagne and caviar."

What Melinda said was true. He wouldn't—couldn't—feel ashamed. In fact, what shamed him now was that he'd felt ashamed when Holly first arrived. But he was proud of what he'd accomplished, just as he was proud to be building on what his parents and grandparents had started on Heart Island.

"Beer and pretzels," he agreed with a lift of his shoulders. "That's me."

"Oh, that reminds me," Holly said.

She dashed away only to return a moment later. To her purchases she added a six-pack of Nate's favorite beer. He was left to wonder if she'd acquired a taste for it or if she planned to invite him over at some point during her stay.

She'd already loaded her purchases into the bed of his pickup when he met her outside a moment later.

They didn't take the "shortcut" this time. Nate took the main roads out to the cabin. They had to stop along the way to let a lazy doe cross the road. Despite the late hour, the big deer was in no hurry. A moment later, a couple of speckled fawns loped after her.

"It's a wildlife sanctuary through most of here. The deer seem to know it. They're not nearly as skittish as they are on public land where hunters are allowed in the fall."

"I didn't mind waiting. She and her babies were worth a little inconvenience."

"They're something," Nate agreed, pressing the gas pedal. "As often as I see them, I still think so."

"They'd make good subject matter."

"For?"

"A painting. I've never done anything but still life

and landscapes. It would be a challenge to try to capture movement and energy."

Moments later, they arrived at her rental. He helped her carry her bags to the house and then stood at the door. He didn't want to leave.

"If you need anything…" he began.

"I know where you live. I'll send up a white flag on the pole off the deck if I find myself in a fix," she promised on a smile.

White flags symbolized surrender, but he didn't say so. "Well, then…"

"Well…"

He shifted his feet on the small rug just inside the doorway. "Maybe I'll see you around."

"I hope so. I won't be going much of anywhere since I haven't any transportation. Maybe you can stop by when you're not busy with work."

Nate nodded, already planning to clear some time in his schedule.

CHAPTER TEN

EARLY THE next morning, Holly tried her hand at fishing. Before leaving the resort the day before, she'd acquired the necessary license and had purchased a bucketful of bait from the marina. After two hours from her deck, she'd caught nothing but weeds and eventually lost her hook. She set the minnows free before calling it a day. Still, she'd had a good time.

But it only took twenty-four hours of solitude for Holly to start wishing for some company. Not just anyone's company. Nate's.

As much she was enjoying her time alone and as utterly beautiful as she found the bay, each time she looked across its sheltered waters, her gaze was drawn to Nate's cottage. The distance was too far to make out any details beyond the actual structure. But every now and again she thought she caught a flash of reflection from his sliding glass doors and imagined him coming out on the deck and maybe staring across the bay to where she was.

She'd come here seeking peace, thinking it was the place that she longed for. Now she knew differently.

It was the man that she wanted.

She went inside for another glass of iced tea. She'd

bought the powdered mix. All she had to do was add water, which took all the guesswork out of it. But she wasn't sure she liked the taste as much. Imitations rarely measured up to the real thing, she knew.

Looking in the refrigerator, she contemplated what to make for dinner. The evening before she'd gone with a turkey sandwich. Today, she'd made toast for breakfast, slightly burnt once again, and had assembled another sandwich for lunch. The sad fact was, despite her grand illusions when she'd gone to the grocery store, Holly didn't know what else to make or how to use the oven. The home had a gourmet kitchen. What it was missing was a gourmet.

A knock sounded at the door as she reached for the deli meat. She went to answer it with a smile blooming on her lips. Only one person knew where to find her. Sure enough, all six foot three of him was standing on the welcome mat, looking gorgeous.

"Hello, Nate."

He smiled. "I hope I'm not disturbing you."

"Not in the least. Come in. Please." She stepped back and he came inside. He was wearing his usual cargo shorts and a short-sleeved shirt that bore the name of the resort on the front. His hair was tousled from the breeze, the ends bleached blond from the sun. The bridge of his nose and cheeks were slightly pink beneath his tan.

"You need to put on more sunscreen," she said absently. "Your face is a little burned."

He touched one of his cheeks, wrinkled his nose. "I put some on this morning, but never got a chance to reapply it."

"Busy day?"

"Very." He shrugged. "That's the way I prefer it. It means business is good, which in turn means I'm doing something right."

Holly liked that about him. He was a hard worker and not one to take anything for granted. He'd gotten his work ethic from his parents, she knew. That's where she'd gotten her own. They might be royals, but her parents weren't ones to loaf around. They saw it as their job to promote the country and champion worthwhile causes.

"I saw a couple of the big boats leave the marina this morning."

"Yeah. They headed out first thing, eager to make the most of the calm water. It's going to get a little choppy later."

"Is another storm blowing in?"

"No. Just some wind and high waves. Big as those boats are, they wouldn't have any trouble weathering them, but it's best not to take chances."

A week ago, Holly might have agreed. Right now, she wasn't so sure. Sometimes a little risk-taking was worth it.

"So, what brings you by?" she asked.

She didn't realize she was holding her breath while she waited for him to respond until it escaped in a whoosh when he said, "Your mother."

"What?"

"She, um, called about an hour ago. She was a little perturbed that you haven't been in touch and that you are hard to reach." Half his mouth crooked up in a smile. "I got quite an earful."

Holly bet he had.

"I'm sorry for that."

"It's all right. I did my best to reassure her that you're fine. But she, um, wants you to call her as soon as possible. It's a matter of some urgency, according to her."

"Everything is a matter of urgency where my mother is concerned," Holly said dryly.

"But you'll call her, right?"

She sighed. "I've been avoiding doing that."

"Any particular reason?"

His expression was nonchalant, but she thought she detected a bit of challenge in Nate's tone.

She didn't know anything about poker, but she decided to lay out all of her cards. "I've ended my relationship with Phillip."

"Oh."

"Oh?" She folded her arms over her chest. "That's pretty monumental, especially where my mother is concerned. I'm sure she's gotten wind of my decision and is eager to try to talk me out of it."

He shrugged. "Ultimately, it's your choice."

"Yes, it is." Again she felt a surge of power. "My life. My future. My decision."

"Spoken like a true princess." He brushed his knuckles over her cheek.

She fought the urge to shiver. The yearning was back, along with the first hot licks of desire.

"Would you...would you like something cold to drink?" she asked.

"I can't stay."

"Oh."

"Another time?"

She nodded.

He turned to leave, then stopped. "Oh, I got this for you."

It was then she noticed the bag in his hand. Inside was a rudimentary set of watercolors, paintbrushes and a tablet of heavy-weight, cold press paper.

"It's not the best quality," Nate said as she pulled everything out and laid it on the counter. "But it was all I could find at the mercantile. I thought it would give you something to do."

Her heart swelled. Over the years she'd received all manner of pricey gifts, none as precious as this. Just as with the fishing pole, it told her he understood her. He knew her. The real Hollyn Saldani. That was a gift in and of itself.

"Thank you."

"No problem." He pointed toward the window. "That view begs to be painted."

"I don't know that I can do it justice."

"The enjoyment comes from trying," he reminded her, before leaving.

Holly called her mother an hour later and regretted it almost as soon as Olivia came on the line.

"You need to come home at once, Hollyn, and fix things with Phillip."

"There's nothing to fix, Mother," Holly said patiently. "We dated for a while, long enough for me to know that he's not the man I see myself marrying." Her gaze strayed to the countertop, where the painting supplies beckoned. No, indeed, Phillip wasn't the man she wanted to spend her life with.

"Nonsense—"

"No," Holly interrupted. "It's not nonsense. It's a fact. I do not love Phillip. I doubt he loves me. We might be well suited according to you, but my opinion is the one that matters here."

"Hollyn, what in the world has gotten into you?"

The same thing that got into her parents three decades ago when they'd decided to buck convention and get married even though doing so meant going against tradition and public opinion.

"I'm deciding my future."

She hung up on Olivia's sputtering protest.

Unlike the day before, Nate didn't have a reason to stop by Holly's place, but when he took out a small fishing boat late the next morning, he found himself trolling by the front of her cottage. She was on the deck, a makeshift easel set up in front of her as she painted.

"Morning, neighbor!" she called when she spotted him.

"Morning," he replied.

She shaded her eyes from the sun. "Are you coming ashore?"

He hadn't planned to. For that matter, he'd only planned to take the boat out to test its rebuilt motor.

"For a minute." He maneuvered the craft to the dock and secured it before hopping out and heading up to the house.

Holly was wearing a simple cotton dress. The ties of a pink bathing-suit top peeked out from the back of the neck. Her feet were bare, and her legs and arms had picked up a little color during her time on the island.

More than pretty, she looked content. Nate wished he could say he was feeling the same. He'd never been more keyed up. As much as he wanted her, he didn't want to complicate her life.

Keep it casual, he told himself. Keep it light. No strings. No binding ties of any sort.

"You're staring." She dabbed at the paper.

"Just enjoying the view."

"The lake is out there." She pointed with her paint-brush, managing to look prim despite the speckle of blue on her cheek.

Nate let his gaze wander south, taking a deliberate tour of her figure before returning to her face. A little flirting wouldn't hurt. "That's not the view I'm enjoying."

She made a show of rolling her eyes, but her shy smile and rose-tinted cheeks told him she wasn't immune.

"I see that you're making use of the paints I brought yesterday."

"This is my third attempt."

He stepped behind the easel she'd created using the seat of a kitchen stool. She'd begun to fill in the outline of the bay, with dreamy shades of blue and green. His house was across the way, a mere speck on the horizon, but there nonetheless.

"It looks good," he said.

She rinsed her brush and shrugged. "It's been a long time since I last dabbled."

"But you're enjoying yourself."

She beamed a smile at him. "Immensely."

That was all that mattered.

"Relaxation looks good on you." He meant only to squeeze her arm, but his fingers failed to release her and instead he found himself pulling her close.

"I am relaxed. I've slept like a baby the past couple nights," she had to go and tell him.

He settled his hands on her waist. "I haven't been sleeping at all."

She set the paintbrush aside. "I'm sorry to hear that."

"Probably just as well. I think I know what I'd be dreaming about."

"Those are called fantasies, Nathaniel." She slapped his chest and tried to look insulted.

He merely grinned. "Which explains why I've been having them while I'm awake."

Her breath hitched. They both grew serious.

"What are you doing for dinner tonight?" she asked just before he could lean down and kiss her.

"I hadn't thought that far ahead." In fact, he wasn't thinking at all at the moment.

"I have two steaks, as you may recall."

"And my favorite beer." Nate nuzzled her cheek.

"Uh-huh." That sexy hitch was back.

"So, is that an invitation?" he managed to ask.

"It's actually more like the solicitation of a favor."

His brow crinkled in confusion.

"I don't know how to work the grill." He opened his mouth to reply, but she put her hand over his lips. "If you're going to say I told you so or make some sort of comment about my being helpless, you can save your breath."

He pulled her hand from his mouth, kissed the palm.

"I wouldn't dream of it."

Indeed, Nate couldn't help thinking that if anyone were helpless here, it was he.

He was back that evening just after six o'clock. He didn't question his decision, though he did question his sanity. Phillip or no Phillip, he kept reminding himself there was only one way this could play out once Holly's time on the island came to an end. Long-distance love affairs were hard enough to manage without all the baggage theirs would come with, assuming that was even what she wanted.

But he decided he didn't care. Bottom line: he wanted Holly. And if he could only have her for a brief time, then he'd have to be content with that. So, he'd showered, shaved for the second time that day and then slapped on some cologne.

His parents called just as he was heading out, both of them on extensions so they could all talk at once. When he'd casually mentioned that Holly was on Heart, his father had sighed. His mother, meanwhile, had grown oddly quiet. He'd expected her to pepper him with questions. The only thing she said after regaining her voice was, "Be careful, son."

He'd laughed. "Be careful. Mom, she's a princess, not an ax murderer."

His mother hadn't laughed. "I know how you felt about her before."

"We both do," his father had added.

"Just…be careful."

"You don't have to worry about me," Nate had assured them. Now, as he followed Holly out onto the deck, he wasn't so sure.

She'd changed into a sleeveless, pale yellow dress whose ruffled front was set in perpetual motion thanks to the breeze. The wind had kicked up since the morning, as the weather forecasters had predicted. The bay was now dotted with whitecaps, and waves crashed at the shore rather than gently rolling onto the sand.

He felt a bit like those waves, set into motion by forces outside his control. Tugged and pulled by fate and the beautiful woman who was now handing him a cold beer that she'd pulled from the bucket of ice on the deck.

"I trust you don't need a glass."

"Nope. Straight from the bottle's fine." He unscrewed the top and helped himself to a long swallow.

She followed suit. "For me, too."

Because he wanted to kiss her, he took a step back instead. "Did you finish your painting?"

She shook her head. Her hair was clipped back at her nape, so the movement of a pair of drop earrings caught his attention.

"Some things take time," she said.

And patience, which had never been Nate's long suit, especially where Holly was concerned. He was a grown man, yet he felt just as he had all those summers ago, desperate to kiss her, wanting to make love to her.

"Are you hungry?"

"Starving." And steak was going to have to do. He set the beverage aside and eyed the huge, stainless steel gas grill. "That's some monster."

Holly looked alarmed. "Does that mean you don't know how to work it, either?"

He laughed, and the sexual frustration he was feeling ebbed to a tolerable level. "I'm a guy, Holly. Guys are born knowing how to grill. I think I read somewhere that it's hardwired into our genetic code."

A couple of minutes later, he had the thing fired up. He found Holly in the kitchen making a salad to go with the steaks.

"I'm afraid this won't be much of a meal. I didn't think to buy any rice or potatoes while I was at the market. And the truth is I wouldn't know how to prepare them either. Apparently the rudiments of meal preparation are not hardwired into my genetic code."

"The rolls you bought are fine."

She pulled a face. "You're just saying that to make me feel better."

He grinned. "Is it working?"

"Somewhat."

"The salad looks good."

"Yes, well, it doesn't require much skill to shred a head of lettuce."

"You had to dice up the tomatoes," he pointed out.

She smiled at that and her hands stilled. She leaned her hip against the counter after she turned to face him. "You know, I think I would enjoy cooking."

"So take it up."

Nate half expected her to shrug off the idea. The woman who had arrived on the island mere days ago would have. She'd seen herself as powerless, a prisoner of fate. The confident woman standing before him now replied, "You know, I think I will." Her expression turned thoughtful. "I could hire someone to teach me or even ask the head chef for some lessons. The palace has excellent kitchen facilities."

Nate's heart sank a little as he pictured her in a great, cavernous kitchen with a Cordon Bleu-trained chef offering instruction, so far away from him compared to the woman who now stood barefoot in this kitchen with a dishtowel wrapped around her waist and an open beer sitting within arm's reach.

"Nate?"

He realized he must have been frowning and shook off his sudden melancholy. "I'd better get those steaks on the grill."

They dined on the deck, taking care to keep track of their napkins, lest the breeze carry them away. As it was, it had made off with a couple pieces of lettuce from Holly's plate, pushing them across the glass tabletop before dumping them in Nate's lap. They'd both laughed.

Holly finished off the last of her steak and sat back on a satisfied sigh. Oh, how she wished she could bottle up this contentment.

"This is what I missed the most," she said quietly. "This…this normalcy."

"We're nothing if not normal around these parts," Nate teased. He grew serious then, set his knife and fork aside and gave her his undivided attention. "What constitutes normal back in Morenci?"

She exhaled slowly. "Well, I don't have an actual job, but I do have a full schedule most days. Awards to present, public appearances to make, ribbons to cut, that sort of thing. Three days a week I make time for my pet projects."

"The charities and causes you've chosen to champion."

"Exactly."

"It sounds like you're very busy."

"I don't mind. At least I feel useful, like I have a purpose. But I rarely get to be myself. To sit beside a lake with a handsome...friend and just relax." She shook her head. "It's ironic."

"What is?"

"My mother was a small-town girl who dreamed of wearing a crown. I'm a princess who dreams of being a small-town girl."

Olivia's dream had come true. She'd made it work despite the obstacles in the beginning that threatened to doom her relationship with Holly's father. Holly remembered her grandmother once saying that neither Morenci nor the king knew what hit them after Olivia arrived for a pageant there three decades earlier. *Indomitable*— that was the word the media often used in reference to the queen. Now, Holly was realizing the apple hadn't fallen very far from the tree.

"I can be myself here." She reached over to cover his hand with hers. "I can be myself with you. I think that is what brought me back here in the first place."

"I'm glad you're here."

She swallowed, felt the need to ask, "Will you still feel that way when Hank comes to collect me in a week?"

It was the great white elephant between them. Yet she was relieved when he chose to ignore it.

"Let's not talk about a week from now." His expression clouded, but the corners of his mouth rose in a wry smile. "As I said before, let's just deal with the here and now."

"I've never been much for living in the moment," she admitted.

"Neither have I. I've always set goals, made plans." She watched his Adam's apple bob just before he said, "But sometimes you just have to take what you can get when you can get it. So, I'm going to sit on this fabulous deck this evening, with an especially beautiful woman, drink another cold beer and enjoy the present."

Her heart rejoiced, even as it broke a little. The future was too much to consider. The here and now was within reach. Holly intended to grab it and hold on tight.

"So, you're going to sit in that chair and enjoy another beer, hmm?"

"I did mention that I would be doing so in the company of a beautiful woman."

"Especially beautiful is, I believe, how you phrased it."

"Glad to know you were paying attention."

"So, you're just going to sit?" she said again.

One of his brows rose. "Is there something else I should be doing?"

She couldn't resist teasing him. "Well, the plates need a scrub. Back home, I have people to do that for me."

"We've already established that you're not back home and that on my island, you're just plain old Holly." He pushed his dirty plate toward her on the tabletop. "I believe I saw a dishwasher in that fancy kitchen, so your manicure is safe. It will do the heavy lifting for you.

All you've got to do is load the thing, add a bit of detergent and push Start."

"Hmm. It sounds rather complicated. Maybe you could show me? I'm a visual learner. I can read or hear instructions a million times and not understand, but if I see something demonstrated just once, well, I'm a natural."

His eyes narrowed. "You don't say?"

"Truly."

"Then, by all means, let me demonstrate."

They both rose and went inside, carrying their plates and utensils with them. But the demonstration Nate had in mind had nothing to do with the pedestrian chore of loading a dishwasher. Thank God! As soon as they reached the kitchen and their plates were on the counter, he pulled Holly into his arms.

"I've been wanting to kiss you since I arrived," he confessed.

"I've been wanting you to kiss me since then."

"Then we're of a like mind."

"I would say so."

Gone was some of the awkwardness they'd experienced before. Holly had come into her own. She wound her arms around his neck and pressed her mouth to his before he could say another word.

Their mouths met, their bodies molded tightly together. Perfect, Holly thought. No one else could fit her so perfectly. His mouth was hot against her. His need and seeming desperation rivaled her own.

I love you, she thought. *I've always loved you. I always will.*

But she reminded herself to live in the moment. No

planning. No future dreams. Just right now. And right now she was feeling not just needy, but greedy.

She had his attention when her fingers began working the buttons on the front of his shirt. He pulled back enough to look down at her hands and then back at her in question. *Are you sure,* those gorgeous dark eyes asked.

"I want you, Nate."

With those simple words, everything changed, including their positions. Somehow she wound up underneath him on the living room's plush sectional. His mouth was hot against her throat, his hands tugging at the dress's sash belt.

"Let me," she said. But the strip of fabric was good and knotted. "I think I saw kitchen sheers in one of the drawers. Or a butcher knife," she panted. "A butcher knife could slice through this silk."

Nate's laughter rumbled low. Holly felt its vibration more than she heard it. "I take it you're not concerned about the outfit then?"

"Let's just say I have other things on my mind than fashion," she managed to reply.

"Good." A moment later she heard a rending of fabric. The belt gave way. "Problem solved," Nate said, helping her up so he could push the dress off her shoulders.

Holly became suddenly shy. She'd never been with a man. Not like this. She'd fooled around some. She was human, after all. But she'd learned early that boys could kiss and tell. And not just their friends and classmates, but any reporter eager for a story about Princess Hollyn. Even with Phillip, she'd held back, mostly because his touches and kisses had done little to ignite her passion. Indeed, for a while, she'd wondered if maybe she was just one of those women who didn't feel much passion. Not frigid exactly, but, well, indifferent.

Well, she wasn't feeling indifferent now. Desperate, needy, maybe even a little depraved given the direction of her thoughts, but definitely not indifferent.

"Something's wrong."

"Nothing's wrong," she disagreed.

"You're quiet."

"Am I supposed to be loud?" she asked.

Nate frowned. "Have…have you ever…"

Embarrassed, she pushed him away so she could sit. "I'm not completely inexperienced."

"Okay." He settled onto the cushion next to her and grabbed her hand. "But have you done…this?"

"I'm twenty-five, Nate."

"Answer the question, Holly."

"If I say no, is it going to change anything?" she asked.

His answer was an emphatic, "Hell, yes!"

Not exactly what she wanted to hear. She started to rise, but he pulled her back to the couch. He cupped her face, kissed her tenderly.

"You didn't let me finish. Yes, it's going to make a difference."

"Why?" she asked.

"Because I'll be sure to take my time."

CHAPTER ELEVEN

I SHOULD regret this, Nate thought as he watched Holly sleep. But he regretted nothing. Even the fact that in a week she would disappear from his life, likely forever.

At least this time he would know why and would know it was coming. Maybe that would make it easier to accept.

She stirred, mumbled something in her sleep. The evening before, she'd surprised him, and not only with her inexperience, but also with the passion she possessed despite that. She was his, he thought with an astounding amount of possessiveness. No matter where fate took them, she would always be his.

He glanced at the clock. Already, the sun was up and light was flooding through the French doors that led to the master suite's second-floor balcony. He didn't want the day to start. He wanted even less to leave her. But some things couldn't be wished away and his livelihood was one of them.

He eased his arm from beneath her. She stirred just as he swung his legs over the side of the mattress.

"Are you going?"

"I've got work to do."

"Will you be back?"

Today for sure. Tonight? Oh, yeah. It was only beyond this week that neither could offer any guarantees. "You mentioned something about chicken breasts."

"I bought a couple at the market, yes."

"I'll bring something to pair them with and we'll make them on the grill."

"You never did show me how to work the dishwasher," she reminded him. She stretched languidly and it was all Nate could do not to climb back into bed with her. The resort be damned.

But he mustered up some resolve. "It can wait until later." He leaned down and nuzzled her neck, feeling overly protective and oddly vulnerable. "I won't be too long."

"See that you aren't."

How was a man supposed to ignore a request like that? And coming from royalty no less? Nate rushed through his day, preoccupied and, okay, a little high on life. He'd had sex before, but he'd never made love. There was a definite difference.

Thank goodness for Mick. He kept Nate from making a monumental mistake on the bill for one of the yacht slips. Nate's misplaced decimal point could have cost Haven a bundle.

"Where's your head, boy?" the older man asked. His smile suggested he knew.

"Sorry."

"She's a pretty one. Are you heading over to see her again tonight?"

Not much got past the old man.

"As soon as I can."

"Why not be on your way now, then? I can finish up

here." Mick added, "And I'll probably be a darn sight more accurate with the receipts than you are anyway."

Far from offended, Nate smiled. The older man didn't need to offer twice. "Thanks. I think I will."

One day floated into the next. Holly tried to remember the last time she'd felt so happy and free, but she couldn't. Even her childhood memories on the island were unable to compete. The man made all the difference, she decided, as she rolled over and snuggled against Nate's side.

He opened one sleepy eye briefly and smiled. Just when she thought he'd returned to slumber, she felt a hand stroke her bare hip. It ended at the slope of her breast, his touch growing more insistent.

"You're awake," she accused.

"I'm up, if that's what you're asking." Male laughter followed.

It was dark yet, not quite four in the morning. "Let's go outside."

"Outside?"

"For a swim."

"That bay is cold," he objected.

"Without our suits."

It was all the enticement he needed. Half an hour later they stumbled back inside, shivering and laughing like a couple of loons before they sobered. Then they made love in front of the gas fireplace downstairs. She watched Nate's face in the flickering glow of the flames, determined to memorize his every expression as need overtook reason.

"I love you," she whispered, but far too low for him

to hear. Still, it seemed important to her to say the words aloud. And though she knew she had to let go, that they both needed to step away from the looming precipice, she was overcome with emotion when she thought she heard him whisper the same thing back.

Holly was leaving.

Actually, she'd extended her stay and had remained on Heart the full two weeks of her lease at the cottage. But that didn't matter to Nate. All that mattered now was that, in mere hours, she would be going away. And he knew from previous experience how it felt to lose her.

Oh, he'd told himself to live in the moment, but he knew he'd been a fool. He was in love with Holly. How could any man watch the woman he loved walk away and not grieve?

The sky was impossibly blue on this day. Nary a cloud breached its perfection. It might as well have been overcast or crowded with thunderclouds. That would have better suited Nate's dark mood as he sat on her deck and waited for Hank's Cessna to swoop out of the sky.

She was equally as quiet as she sat on a lounge chair beside him. He knew her thoughts as well as his own, which was why he didn't try to stop her or urge her to stay a little longer. They'd been on borrowed time as it was. They'd both known that going in.

The Cessna came into view. Hank dipped the wings in greeting as he passed and then circled back for a landing. The floats skimmed off the water's surface once before touching down for good.

"He's right on time," Nate remarked quietly.

"Yes. At least this trip should be less eventful," Holly noted.

Hank taxied the seaplane toward the dock. Nate went out to help him, grabbing the rope the other man threw to him.

"Hey, Nate. Gorgeous day, huh?"

A grumble served as his reply.

Hank turned to Holly and asked, "All set, pretty lady?"

"Not hardly," she surprised them all by saying. "I wish I could stay…indefinitely." Her gaze was on Nate.

"We both knew you would have to leave." It killed him to say so.

"I'll try to come back soon."

He nodded. They both knew it was a lie. This was it. The end of an otherwise perfect love affair.

Hank went to fetch Holly's bags from the deck, leaving the pair of them to say their goodbyes. Not that they hadn't done so already. Hell, the entire morning had been one long and painful farewell.

"I'll call when I get home."

"Do that," Nate said.

But he knew a moment of doubt. Would she? Once she'd settled into the routine of her other life, would Holly remember to call or even email Nate? Or would her time on Heart Island be filed away as a beautiful memory? Yes, as she'd said, she could be herself here. But the rest of the world expected her to be a princess.

"I've got all your bags stowed," Hank said as he loaded the last of them into the seaplane. "I'll be ready to take off when you are."

"Thank you, Hank."

"I guess this is it," Nate said.

"You make it sound very final," Holly objected.

He exhaled slowly. "It is what it is."

"You don't think I'll be back?"

"I hope you will, but our lives are going to pull us in two different directions," Nate said practically. He wasn't trying to hurt her. Quite the opposite. He wanted to be sure she knew he understood.

"That doesn't mean we have to go in those directions," Holly said. "You're the one who once told me I wasn't without choices and that I needed to make time for the things I felt were important."

Indeed, he had. Yet, he wasn't sure how to respond to her words now.

"Would you come to Morenci if I asked you to?" she said softly.

"I... Would I...?" She'd caught him off guard. "The resort..."

"For a visit, Nate."

He felt foolish. "Sure. I mean, I could swing a week or two, especially in the off-season."

"You love it here," Holly said quietly.

"I love you."

The words were out before he could stop them. He wondered if he would have tried to if given the chance.

Her eyes grew moist. A tear slipped down her cheek. "I love you, too, Nate."

The kiss they shared wasn't as passionate as some of the others had been. No desperate urgency now. But the emotions behind it would stay with Nate a lifetime.

He'd thought he knew what heartbreak felt like. This was total annihilation.

The pressure only grew worse as he helped her board the plane. The door slammed shut as his own eyes watered and her image grew blurry. He pushed the plane away from the dock. The prop revved to life, the sound intensifying long before the plane actually moved. He stepped back and waited where he was as it glided over the calm water of the bay, picking up speed as it left Nate and the shore behind.

He raised a hand and waved just as the floats left the water's smooth surface. Holly's plane had lifted off safely. Meanwhile, Nate's heart had crashed and burned.

"This weekend is the annual Royal Gala," her mother was saying. "You're cutting it close with your late arrival. Luckily, Anna is standing by," Olivia said of the royal seamstress. "You'll need a final fitting on your gown."

"Yes."

Olivia plucked at Holly's sun-bleached curls. "And you probably should have your hair treated. A good deep conditioning is in order. It looks dry."

"Yes."

Her agreement did little to assuage Olivia.

"Is something wrong?"

"What could be wrong? I'm back where I belong, doing what needs to be done," Holly reminded her.

"Yes, but you're...so unhappy."

"I've *been* unhappy, Mother."

"But not like this," Olivia replied. "I've never seen you like this."

Which made sense, since Holly had never felt like this. It had been all well and good to tell Nate that they would live in the moment while they were living in the moment. Now that the moment was over, the pain was almost too much to bear.

"Mother, did Gran ever try to talk you out of marrying my father?"

Olivia blinked in surprise at the question. "Talk me out of it? No. But she was clear on what it would entail. She made sure I went into it with my eyes wide open and then backed me all the way as I fought like a tiger cat to fit in and be accepted, especially once you were on the way."

"That must have been hard for you."

"At first." Olivia sucked in a breath. "It was one thing for them not to accept me. I wouldn't allow them to turn their backs on you. You're the throne's rightful heir, after all."

"And if I don't want it?"

Olivia's footsteps echoed to a halt in the long corridor. She snagged Holly's arm, forcing her to stop as well. "My God! You're in love with that boy."

"He's a man now. But yes. I love Nate Matthews. I loved him when I was a girl and I love him now."

"But...you can't mean you want to turn your back on everything I've worked so hard to ensure you had. You're accepted here, Hollyn. No one dares question your right to ascend the throne, not like they did with me."

"That was important to you."

"Very," Olivia replied. "That's why I've done all that I have."

She hugged her mother. "Thank you for that, Mother. Truly, thank you. But I'm happiest being...ordinary."

Olivia hugged her back fiercely before pulling away. Holding Holly at arm's length, she said, "But you're not ordinary."

Holly closed her eyes in defeat. As soon as she did, she felt her mother's lips press to her cheek. "When a woman is in love, she's...extraordinary," Olivia whispered.

CHAPTER TWELVE

"How are the day's receipts looking?" Nate asked Mick as he came in the marina.

"Better than you do," the older man remarked.

And wasn't that the truth.

Holly had been gone two days. It might as well have been ten years. God, Nate missed her. He ached with it. He'd slept with the phone by his side the first night, eager for her call. It hadn't come.

"One of the Burns boys took a phone message about an hour ago," Mick was saying. Nate's heart soared until the older man added, "I spilled my coffee on it, but it looks to be an invite to meet for drinks at the Fishing Hole when you get out of work."

Probably one of his poker buddies. They usually called him up when they were running low on funds and hoping for someone to buy a round. Well, he had no plans to indulge them.

He put in a couple more hours before calling it a day. And what a day it had been. Though it wasn't exactly in his job description, he'd helped change the prop on a slip owner's fishing boat. He'd also spent a couple of hours teaching some of the resort's youngest guests the finer points of baiting a hook. Despite a good scrubbing, he still smelled a little bit like diesel fuel and the water in the big filtered tank where they stored the minnows.

He started for home, but pointed the truck in the direction of town instead. The invitation from friends beckoned. There was nothing waiting for him at home. And no one. He'd wind up staring at the phone again, willing the damned thing to ring. The pub, on the other hand, would be full of friendly and familiar faces, cold beer and banal conversation. That's what he needed.

He got a whole lot more the moment he stepped through the pub's door. He spotted Holly.

She was impossible to miss. And not because she was the only woman in the place wearing a skirt and looking like she could grace the pages of a fashion magazine. No, she was standing atop the pool table and, from what he could gather, leading the crowd of locals in a line dance to an Alan Jackson song. It was a bit of the traditional boot-scooting he'd taught her way back when with what appeared to be some Celtic footwork thrown in.

Lord of the Dance at a hoedown?

Damned diesel fumes. They had him seeing things. He rubbed his eyes. But the image didn't go away, and he wasn't sure he wanted it to. He became mesmerized watching the hem of Holly's skirt as it flitted back and forth just above her knees with each shake of her hips and flick of her feet. Then her gaze found his and her footsteps faltered before she stumbled to a stop. Her already flushed cheeks turned all but crimson.

"That's all I know," she shouted apologetically when the crowd of mostly locals started to grumble.

Melinda from the grocery store was among them and the first to offer Holly a hand down from the table.

Since Holly had already seen him, it was only polite to go over and say hello. Under other circumstances, he might have offered to buy her a drink, but he had a feeling she'd already had one too many. Oddly enough, when he reached the table where she sat, Holly was sipping from a glass of plain old cola. The remnants of what appeared to be the pub's famous bacon and cheddar-loaded potato skins were on a platter in front of her.

"Hello, Nate." Holly pushed out the extra chair with her foot as an invitation for him to join them. "I was wondering if you got my message."

"I... Mick spilled coffee on it. I wasn't sure who it was from," Nate admitted.

"Hmm." She frowned. "But you came anyway."

"I wanted a beer."

She smiled around her straw. "And now? Is that all you want?"

"I..." *Hold on to some pride*, he ordered himself. "What are you doing here?"

"Well, I was dancing." Holly set her beverage aside. "For the record, I was dared."

As much as Nate wanted answers, he laughed. At the absurdity of the statement as much as the ridiculous amount of dignity she managed to muster in uttering it. "Gee, it makes perfect sense now why I should find you on a pool table in a pub doing a tush-push when I thought you were back in Morenci."

In a way, it did make sense. Holly never could turn down a dare. She reminded him of that now.

"You know I've come to hate being predictable. It's nice to shake things up a little every now and then. I believe that's the expression."

"Uh-huh." But Nate was sure of little else at the moment.

Holly went on. "The man standing next to the jukebox was a little surly with me at first." She pointed to the big hulking man most locals left alone. "He told me they don't play any opera in here. I think he was just having a little fun with me."

Nate glanced over to where she pointed. Actually, Zeb Barlow probably hadn't been teasing. The island's only mechanic had a bad attitude when it came to tourists, especially those who looked the part, which Holly definitely did wearing a skirt, sexy sandals and a pearl necklace. She might as well have had on a tiara. Jeans and sneakers were dress code here—or, in Zeb's case, stained brown coveralls and steel-toed boots.

"I told him I wasn't interested in a night at the opera. I was looking for some proper dance music," Holly said.

Despite the fact he was dying for an explanation, Nate's lips twitched at her *proper* tone. "I bet that went over well."

"He dared me to show him my best moves. So, I was. It was the bartender's idea that I get up on the pool table to do it. And then people just started joining in and asking me to show them more. I threw in a toe kick I learned in the Celtic step class Mother insisted I take, and the next thing I knew I was leading a line dance."

She sounded amazed. And a little proud.

"You're here," he said. He stroked her arm, just to

be sure she wasn't a figment of his imagination. Soft skin warmed his fingers.

"I'm here." Her smile wobbled.

He cleared his throat and pulled his hand back. "For, um, how long this time?"

"I'm not sure yet," she admitted.

His bruised heart took a tumble.

The waitress came by and cleared away the empty potato skins tray, as well as a couple of empty drink glasses.

"Can I get you anything, Nate?" she asked.

"Whatever you've got on tap is fine, and another drink for the lady."

"Nothing for me," Holly corrected.

"You still haven't told me why you're here."

"I should think that would be obvious."

Under normal circumstances and with another woman, perhaps, it might have been. Tonight, here, with Holly, Nate's brain felt fuzzy and too slow to comprehend. And his heart was just a little too battered to hope.

"Let's get out of here," he said. "It's too loud to talk."

But she shook her head. "In a minute. I have one more dance. Maybe you'll join me for this one."

She marched to the jukebox and inserted a dollar bill before pressing some buttons. God only knew what line dance she would be leading the pub patrons in next. He had no plans to join her.

Zeb strolled over and commented, "She's a pretty little thing."

"She's mine," Nate shot back. And dammit if he wasn't going to make sure she knew it. Whatever the obstacles, they'd figure them out. They'd make this work, because nothing in his life worked without her.

He pushed to his feet as the first strains of music filled the bar. No country twang or do-si-do beat. Rather, Van Halen's power ballad "When It's Love."

Nate grinned as he recognized the tune. That last morning, he'd been humming it in the shower while he'd washed her back…and then her front.

"I'll make a hard rock fan of you yet," he'd teased.

Apparently, he had.

The crowd around him melted into an indistinguishable kaleidoscope of colors and shapes as he made his way to Holly. She was smiling.

"It's kind of catchy," she said when he reached her. "Although not the easiest to dance to."

"Maybe I'll just stand here and hold you in my arms then."

"Suits me," she replied as he slipped his left arm around her waist and scooped up her right hand in his.

Holly settled her cheek against his and sighed.

"About the length of your visit this time," he began. He wasn't going to take a week or ten days or so for an answer. It turned out he didn't need to.

"I was thinking I'd stay…forever."

He stopped moving and pulled back so he could see her face. "Holly?"

"I love you, Nate."

"And I love you. But—"

She put her fingers over his mouth. "No buts. That's where it ends."

"You're wrong." He kissed the hand he planned to put a wedding ring on as soon as he could manage it. "This is where it begins."

EPILOGUE

HOLLYN Elise Phillipa Saldani had been born a princess. Three years after her return to Heart, she was a bona fide islander with a new name. The locals not only had accepted Holly Matthews as Nate's bride, but they also fiercely protected her from the prying eyes of outsiders, whether they be paparazzi, traditional journalists or merely nosy tourists.

For the most part, Holly found that while people—including guests at the resort—were often curious about her, they mostly left her alone. Especially now that the uproar over her decision to abdicate her claim on Morenci's throne had died down.

Her cousin Amelia had been only too happy to take Holly's place. As much as Holly had chafed under the public spotlight, Amelia seemed to enjoy it. And while Holly's parents weren't exactly thrilled with her decision, they respected it.

And they had accepted Nate.

Three years married to a man she loved so deeply had confirmed one thing: her mother was right. No woman in love was ordinary.

Nor was a woman expecting her first child. Holly

touched her stomach in wonder. She still couldn't believe it. She was nearly three months along.

Nate jogged out to where she stood on the marina dock. Worry creased his forehead. She hadn't been feeling well lately, which was why he'd insisted she go see the doctor.

"Mick said you needed to see me right away. Everything go okay at your appointment?"

"Better than okay." She handed him the grainy black-and-white ultrasound photo. "They said it's still too early to tell if it's a girl or a boy."

"A b-baby?" Nate eyed her blankly for a moment before his disbelief finally ebbed. Then he scooped her up in his arms on a whoop of joy. "We're going to have a baby!" he shouted to no one in particular.

He tripped on one of the mooring lines. Just as he had that day three years ago when he'd tried to carry her to shore, he lost his footing. They both wound up going off the side of the dock into the water.

They came up laughing, wrapped together.

"Looks like we're in over our heads," Nate said on a grin.

Holly grinned back. "I wouldn't have it any other way."

* * * * *

CLASSIC

Quintessential, modern love stories
that are romance at its finest.

COMING NEXT MONTH
AVAILABLE DECEMBER 6, 2011

#4279 KISSES ON HER CHRISTMAS LIST
Susan Meier

#4280 RUNAWAY BRIDE
Changing Grooms
Barbara Hannay

#4281 FAMILY CHRISTMAS IN RIVERBEND
Shirley Jump

#4282 FLIRTING WITH ITALIAN
Liz Fielding

#4283 NIKKI AND THE LONE WOLF
Banksia Bay
Marion Lennox

#4284 THE SECRETARY'S SECRET
Michelle Douglas

You can find more information on upcoming Harlequin® titles,
free excerpts and more at www.HarlequinInsideRomance.com.

HRCNM1111

REQUEST YOUR FREE BOOKS!
2 FREE NOVELS PLUS 2 FREE GIFTS!

❖Harlequin®

Romance

From the Heart, For the Heart

*Lucy Flemming and Ross Mitchell shared a magical,
sexy Christmas weekend together six years ago.
This Christmas, history may repeat itself when they find
themselves stranded in a major snowstorm...
and alone at last.*

Read on for a sneak peek from
IT HAPPENED ONE CHRISTMAS
by Leslie Kelly.

Available December 2011, only from Harlequin® Blaze™.

EYEING THE GRAY, THICK SKY through the expansive wall of windows, Lucy began to pack up her photography gear. The Christmas party was winding down, only a dozen or so people remaining on this floor, which had been transformed from cubicles and meeting rooms to a holiday funland. She smiled at those nearest to her, then, seeing the glances at her silly elf hat, she reached up to tug it off her head.

Before she could do it, however, she heard a voice. A deep, male voice—smooth and sexy, and so not Santa's.

"I appreciate you filling in on such short notice. I've heard you do a terrific job."

Lucy didn't turn around, letting her brain process what she was hearing. Her whole body had stiffened, the hairs on the back of her neck standing up, her skin tightening into tiny goose bumps. Because that voice sounded so familiar. *Impossibly* familiar.

It can't be.

"It sounds like the kids had a great time."

Unable to stop herself, Lucy began to turn around, wondering if her ears—and all her other senses—were deceiving her. After all, six years was a long time, the mind could play tricks. What were the odds that she'd bump into *him,* here? And today of all days. December 23.

Six years exactly. Was that really possible?

One look—and the accompanying frantic thudding of her heart—and she knew her ears and brain were working just fine. Because it was *him.*

"Oh, my God," he whispered, shocked, frozen, staring as thoroughly as she was. "Lucy?"

She nodded slowly, not taking her eyes off him, wondering why the years had made him even more attractive than ever. It didn't seem fair. Not when she'd spent the past six years thinking he must have started losing that thick, golden-brown hair, or added a spare tire to that trim, muscular form.

No.

The man was gorgeous. Truly, without-a-doubt, mouth-wateringly handsome, every bit as hot as he'd been the first time she'd laid eyes on him. She'd been twenty-two, he one year older.

They'd shared an amazing holiday season.

And had never seen one another again.

Until now.

Find out what happens in
IT HAPPENED ONE CHRISTMAS
by Leslie Kelly.
Available December 2011, only from Harlequin® Blaze™

Harlequin® *Romance*

SUSAN MEIER

*Experience the thrill of falling in love
this holiday season with*

Kisses on Her Christmas List

When Shannon Raleigh saw Rory Wallace staring at her
across her family's department store, she knew he would
be trouble…for her heart. Guarded, but unable to fight
her attraction, Shannon is drawn to Rory and his inquisitive
daughter. Now with only seven days to convince this
straitlaced businessman that what they feel for each other
is real, Shannon hopes for a Christmas miracle.

**Will the magic of Christmas be enough
to melt his heart?**

Available December 6, 2011.

www.Harlequin.com

HR17769

LAURA MARIE ALTOM
brings you
another touching tale from

When family tragedy forces Wyatt Buckhorn to pair up
with his longtime secret crush, Natalie Poole, and care
for the Buckhorn clan's seven children, Wyatt worries
he's in over his head. Fearing his shameful secret will
be exposed, Wyatt tries to fight his growing attraction
to Natalie. As Natalie begins to open up to Wyatt,
he starts yearning for a family of his own—a family
with Natalie. But can Wyatt trust his heart enough
to reveal his secret?

A Baby in His Stocking

Available December
wherever books are sold!